Mary Elizabeth Braddon

Dead Men's Shoes

Vol. II

Mary Elizabeth Braddon

Dead Men's Shoes
Vol. II

ISBN/EAN: 9783337050658

Printed in Europe, USA, Canada, Australia, Japan

Cover: Foto ©Andreas Hilbeck / pixelio.de

More available books at **www.hansebooks.com**

DEAD MEN'S SHOES

A Novel

BY THE AUTHOR OF

'LADY AUDLEY'S SECRET'

ETC. ETC. ETC.

IN THREE VOLUMES

VOL. II.

LONDON

JOHN MAXWELL AND CO.

4, SHOE LANE, FLEET STREET

1876

CONTENTS TO VOL. II.

DEAD MEN'S SHOES.

———◆———

CHAPTER I.

A DANGEROUS TRIUMPH.

THAT visit of Sir Wilford Cardonnel's to Lancaster
Lodge is followed in about ten days by a second
morning call, the baronet being supported on this
occasion by his elder sister, a rather strong-minded
young woman, who rejoices in the pastoral name of
Phœbe.

'My sisters are dying to know you,' says Sir
Wilford, with a gush of enthusiasm, after the necessary introductions have been gone through in a
slipshod way, Sir Wilford being careless of the
rules and ceremonies of polite life.

Miss Cardonnel's countenance does not support her brother's statement by any gleam of light from the spirit within. She is looking round the handsome—upholsterer's—drawing-room with a critical air, taking stock of the big Japanese vases, so like those in the window of the chief grocer at Krampston, the crimson satin curtains, and sofas, half an acre or so of looking-glass, the black boys in front of the console table, holding up golden baskets of emptiness in their ebony arms. A room so different from the spacious saloon at the How, with its faded curtains and fine old pictures, its tulipwood coffee-tables and threadbare carpets, its crystal chandeliers, and cabinets of old English china, collected by the grandmothers and great-grandmothers of the reigning family.

'What a pity these commercial people have everything so fine and so new!' thinks Miss Cardonnel. 'If they didn't burst out into all this splendour one might forget they were parvenus. The girl is pretty, I suppose, or what most people call pretty. Features too sharply cut for my taste.'

Miss Cardonnel's features are of the blunt order,

and her face inclines to that type of beauty which the vulgar mind classifies as 'puddingy.'

They have found Sibyl in the drawing-room, looking her very prettiest in white muslin, much adorned with Valenciennes, straw-coloured bows dotted about here and there among the flouncings and ruchings, and a broad straw-coloured sash tied with that artistic carelessness which is one of Sibyl's gifts. She has a running account now at Carmichael's, the leading draper of Redcastle, and orders what she likes. The account has been running for the past twelve months, and indulgent as her millionaire uncle is, Sibyl rather dreads the hour when the sum-total of this account shall be brought under his notice. But in a dull provincial town what excitement can a pretty girl have except a little extravagance in the way of dress? Even matrons whose beauty is a matter of tradition are apt to plunge into a vortex of millinery for want of any other whirlpool wherein to rotate.

Stephen Trenchard receives his guests with a marked graciousness, accepts Sir Wilford's friendly advances greedily, and tries to make himself agreeable to Miss Cardonnel, who is rather more stony and unimpressionable than she ought to be if she comes prepared to extend the hand of friendship.

'I am very glad for my niece to make pleasant —indeed distinguished acquaintance,' says Mr. Trenchard. 'People in Redcastle have been very kind, Mrs. Stormont especially, quite motherly in her goodness to Sibyl. But I am better pleased for her to know county people, there is a—a difference.'

'Yes, I suppose you find it so,' replies Miss Cardonnel coolly, as if she felt that she belonged to another order of bipeds. 'Mrs. Stormont is nice, of course,' with seraphic patronage, 'very good family, I believe, the Stormonts,'—this dubiously, as much as to say, 'so they tell me, poor creatures, but I haven't seen the particulars in Burke.'

Sir Wilford has come to ask when Mr. Trenchard is going to drive Miss Faunthorpe over to the How.

'If you want to see our roses, you know, you must not lose any time, you know,' he adds, emphatically,—'must they, Phœbe?'

'The roses are nearly over now, Wilford,' replies

Miss Cardonnel, which remark is not exactly a warm invitation.

'Oh, stuff! why, you were saying that the Dijons were just in their glory this very morning, while we were waiting for the phaeton. When will you come, Miss Faunthorpe? To-morrow—Wednesday —Thursday?'

'We dine at the Friary on Wednesday, Wilford.'

'Ah, to be sure. To-morrow, then?'

Sibyl looks embarrassed. This marked attention from the head of a county family kindles no flush of gratified vanity on her cheek to-day. Sir Wilford's admiration was pleasant enough on the racecourse, a triumph in the sight of all Redcastle, but the matter is now growing more serious. She begins to think that she has really made a conquest, that Sir Wilford is disagreeably in earnest.

'It is like the realization of my childish dream about a rich husband, and all the bells in Redcastle ringing for my wedding,' she says to herself, 'only it comes too late. I am not sorry that it is so. I have no regret. I made my choice, and shall be proud to stand by it when the time comes. Only it is curious that the childish dream should come true after all.'

'Will you come to the How to-morrow, Mr. Trenchard?' asks Sir Wilford. 'We have some old pictures that you may like to see. There's a Vandyke my father used to think great things of, and our gardens are worth a visit in this weather, though I'm always blowing up those beggars of gardeners. Come early, and we can do the gardens before luncheon, and the pictures after.'

'My uncle so seldom goes out in the morning,' says Sibyl, quickly, as if eager to find an excuse for declining.

'But this invitation is too tempting to be refused,' interposes Mr. Trenchard. 'I have heard wonders of the How. Mrs. Stormont is very fond of talking about the How vineries and the How stables.'

'Then you'll come to-morrow,' exclaims Sir Wilford, delightedly.

Miss Cardonnel is lost in contemplation of the lights and shadows on the lawn, seen under the Spanish blind, which affords but a limited view of the garden.

'If that day will suit Miss Cardonnel's engagements.'

'Oh, I shall be very happy, I'm sure,' replies the young lady thus directly appealed to.

After this Miss Cardonnel is tolerably civil, and talks to Sibyl a little, questioning her about her habits and amusements—whether she rides, is fond of croquet, archery, and so on, with rather a district-visiting air, as of a kindly inquirer letting herself down to the level of the lower classes.

'You have a croquet club, or something of that sort in Redcastle,' she says, loftily, as if she had never had the institution clearly explained to her. 'I rather think my sister and I are honorary members, but we've never been.'

'Yes, there is a club for croquet and archery. They meet in Sir John Boldero's park.'

'Very nice for you, I dare say,' remarks Miss Cardonnel, as much as to say, 'People of your class must be provided with amusements of some kind.'

They all take a little stroll in the garden presently, and Miss Cardonnel deigns to admire the fine old plane trees on the lawn. It is a considerable relief to move about in the sunshine, and have flower-beds and standard roses to look at and talk about, after that forced conversation in the drawing-room.

'I think your ribbon borders are better than ours,' remarks Miss Cardonnel. 'Those are the stables, I suppose,' looking at the slated roofs which appear just above the shrubbery. 'Have you many saddle-horses?'

'Only the one my uncle bought for me. The groom rides one of the carriage horses.'

Miss Cardonnel visibly shudders.

'And is your horse nice?'

'She's a darling, very pretty, and very gentle.'

'Indeed,' says Miss Cardonnel. 'I hate gentle horses. I like a horse to be lively, and give me something to do. It must be rather dull work for you riding alone, if you're not particularly fond of riding.'

'Oh, but I'm very fond of riding.'

'You don't hunt, I suppose?'

'No, my uncle would hardly like that, I think.'

'I dare say not. Wilford, your roans must be

very tired of waiting, and I have some more calls to make.'

Mr. Trenchard begs his guests to stay to luncheon.

'Thanks; you are very good, but it would be quite impossible,' replies Miss Cardonnel, decisively. I have so much to do before I go home. Then we are to see you at the How to-morrow. Good-bye. —Come, Wilford, pray.'

Sir Wilford, who has been gazing at Sibyl, and forgetting the engagements of life and time, follows his sister reluctantly, after a cordial leave-taking.

'Well, little woman, I think there's no doubt about your having made a conquest there,' says Stephen Trenchard, directly the Cardonnels have vanished.

His tone is at once more cheerful and more affectionate than it has been for some little time, for a period dating from that night on which he received his nameless visitor.

'Please don't talk about conquests, uncle.'

'Nonsense, child! It's a subject I'm very glad to talk about. I want you to marry well. I should like you to make a brilliant marriage, Sibyl, before I am gone.'

'Dear uncle, pray don't——'

'My love, I'm an old man,—tough and wiry enough, it is true, but well on in years. I can't expect to live for ever. And I should like to see you well placed in life before I say my *nunc dimittis.*'

'What does it matter, uncle?' says Sibyl impatiently.

It is so tiresome of this old man—rolling in wealth, and of course intending to bequeath a considerable portion of his riches to her—to harp thus persistently upon the advantages of a good marriage. What could a rich husband avail to one who is to be so richly dowered? Two fortunes are no better than one if the one be large enough for every earthly desire.

'Believe me, dear uncle, I have no idea of marrying. I never shall marry. And as for Sir Wilford Cardonnel,' adds Sibyl with asperity, 'I positively hate him.'

She has her husband's letter in her bosom—that letter written in the Pimlico coffee-house, and transmitted through Jane Dimond's toil-stained hands,—and the **idea of** any other man's admiration is revolting **to** her. **If—if she** dared but tell her uncle the truth! **If he had not this rooted** hatred **of** his dead enemy's **race, how** different **life might** be!

'Hate **a fine, handsome** young **man—one of the** best **men in** the county—who has come **out of** his **way to pay you** attention! **I'm ashamed of** you, **Sibyl,'** exclaims Stephen Trenchard, **and his** bristling brows contract threateningly over his keen dark eyes as he scrutinizes Sibyl's pale face.

'I hope there is no one else in the background,' he says, '**no** scamp whose acquaintance **you made in London.** Perhaps **that's the** reason why you stayed away so long after I had asked **to see you.'**

Sibyl's pale cheek grows paler.

'**There is no one,** uncle,' **she** says resolutely, feeling that the situation is desperate. 'Have you ever heard me speak of any one? **All** I want is not to be worried about marrying. If you are tired **of** me, **if** you think me an encumbrance, **or a burden,** send me away. I can go back to uncle Robert, or I can **be a** governess again.'

This little bit of temper, or independence, pleases Mr. Trenchard.

'Don't fly into a passion, little one,' he says, kindly. 'I suppose you know how pretty you look when you are angry. I won't tease you any more about getting married, but when a good chance offers don't refuse it. That's all I say, my dear.'

They go in to luncheon together, and Sibyl resumes those pretty coaxing ways that have won her uncle's heart. She sits near him and ministers to his wants, which are not many, never forgets to hand him the Nepaul pepper, pours out his glass of claret—all with a caressing tenderness which is not without its charm for him.

'I think I shall pay a duty visit this afternoon, uncle, unless you want me for anything.'

'Going to see your sister and the old doctor, I suppose,' replies Mr. Trenchard. He speaks of Robert Faunthorpe with a touch of compassion, as if the surgeon were considerably his senior, instead of being his junior by about ten years.

'Yes, uncle. Marion thinks me unkind for not

going oftener. But it's such a long dusty walk through the town, and if I take the carriage she does nothing but sneer at me.'

'Poor Marion,' says Mr. Trenchard. 'She has all the littleness of a girl fresh from boarding school. Let her sneer, child. We must all live our own lives, and let people think what they like about us. You'd better take the carriage.'

'It's not worth while. I should like to stop with Marion and Jenny for a few hours. I shall be back to dinner, of course, uncle.'

'I'm glad of that. You've spoiled me for lonely dinners, little one. I miss those bright eyes of yours at the other side of the table.

It is a broiling summer afternoon, and that long empty street below Bar, the broad bright market-place, Little Bethel, the British schools, the Sunday school, the Independent Chapel, the Athena Lodge, are all glaring in the sun. Mrs. Groshen has made her house-front a blaze of geranium and calceolaria, festoons of verdure hang down from the encaustic flower-boxes, brass canary cages glitter in the open windows. Dr. Mitsand's grave old house on the shady side of the street, brown and sombre, contrasts this variegated glare. From this point the houses decrease in size and importance, and a little lower down begin the shops —all of a refined and elegant character at this end of the street. The hairdresser's—the stationer and bookseller's—the fancy and Berlin wool warehouse —the photographer's—the fashionable pastrycook's, in whose plate-glass window appear a wooden wedding cake, sumptuously decorated with fly-spotted plaster of Paris, two glass jellies, and three tall glass jars of confectionery of the méringue and cracker bonbon order, which have never been opened within the knowledge of the external world. The méringues, the bonbons, the Savoy biscuits are pale with old age. But the confectioner is not without business, for it is he who supplies the *vol au vents à la Financière*, and the lobster cutlets which are an inevitable feature in a Redcastle dinner.

After these genteeler repositories come the vulgar every-day butchers and bakers, grocers, candlestick-makers, drapers, and tallow-chandlers.

The street opens into the market square, in the middle of which stands the town hall, square and imposing, with a façade of no particular style, and a big-faced clock which is always at variance with the minster. Here, too, is the police station at a corner, with a flaming bill stuck against its stony front, offering a reward for the apprehension of the assassin in a murder case which no one has ever heard of. That bill will disappear in a day or two, and no one in Redcastle will ever be any the wiser about the murderer or murder. After the market square the high street, or main artery of the town, dwindles and grows narrow. The shops become dingy and small. There are rows of cottages at intervals; then a row of very ancient and shabby almshouses, whose parlours have sunk below the level of the pavement, and whose upper chambers are no higher than the passing pedestrian's shoulder. Here, at the end of the street, the centre of all this shabbiness, rising sublimely above the petty modern town, stands the minster—one of the most perfect cathedral churches in the land,—its ancient burial-ground stretching widely behind it, a forge and a cluster of old-fashioned cottages for its opposite neighbours, and beyond the white high road and the open fields. There are a few houses and gardens on this high road, and the second of these, on the same side as the minster, is Dr. Faunthorpe's dull old dwelling. The roses are in bloom in the front garden to-day, and brighten the aspect of the house a little, but the roses and the grass, the old cherry tree in the corner, and the jessamine against the wall are all alike whitened with dust.

The garden gate is rarely locked, and the house door is always open in warm weather, so Sibyl has nothing to do but walk in. She has not seen her relatives at this end of the town since she saw them on the racecourse, and she is quite prepared to find Marion somewhat cantankerous. That young lady starts up from the sofa with flushed face, rumpled hair, and a generally towzled appearance, as Sibyl enters the every-day parlour. She has fallen asleep over a novel, in which an impossibly lovely and accomplished heroine revolves in a circle of dukes and duchesses, marquises and millionaires; the male members of which patrician society fall in love with her at the slightest provocation.

'Oh!' exclaims Marion, with a long yawn, 'It's you, is it? I didn't expect you'd come and see *us* any more, now that you've made the acquaintance of the county. Pray to what fortuitous combination of circumstances do we owe this unlooked-for honour?' she adds, with a touch of the all-accomplished heroine's dignity.

'Don't be an idiot, Marion. I wonder I ever do come to see you, considering how execrable you make yourself.'

'I do not enjoy *your* opportunities,' replies Marion, briskly.' *I* am not favoured with the friendship of the Stormonts. *I* don't live in a splendidly furnished house with pampered flunkeys to wait upon me. *I* haven't a running account at the draper's. In short, I'm a low vulgar person altogether.'

'Marion, you are too absurd!'

'"Her manners had not the repose that marks the cast of Vere de Vere."' You ought to pity my shortcomings. I dare say when you are Lady Cardonnel you will cut me altogether. You looked as if you would have liked to do it on the racecourse.'

'And so I should, you provoking minx. The idea of taking that horrid old rattle-trap of a pony carriage up to the racecourse, to let all Redcastle see how often the harness has been mended, and how the cushions have been devoured by moths!'

'Everybody can't have barouches and pairs,' cries Marion, with vixenish energy. 'You thought I was going to stay away from the races, did you? while you were enjoying yourself with your grand friends. If you didn't want me to go in uncle Robert's pony chaise, why didn't you take me in uncle Trenchard's barouche? He's my uncle every bit as much as he's yours, unless I'm a changeling. I was to be moping at home, was I, while you were decked out in new bonnets and things, and flirting audaciously with a baronet. Cinderella's sisters were kindness itself compared with you.'

'Talk as much nonsense as you like, Marion, I'm not going to quarrel with you. The weather's much too warm for family squabbles. I'm sure I've been nearly melted between Lancaster Lodge and here.'

'People accustomed to a barouche must find walking a trial.'

'Where's Jenny?'

'Making an object of herself in the garden, I suppose,' replies Marion, flinging herself down upon the sofa and resuming her novel.

'I'll go and have a chat with her. She's pleasanter company than you are, at any rate.'

'I dare say,' says Marion contemptuously, with her back to her sister. 'Some people don't like home truths.'

Sibyl goes into the garden, not displeased at being on bad terms with Marion. Jenny is the person she has come to see, and it is vital to her to see Jenny alone.

The long old-fashioned garden is a land flowing with milk and honey in this blazing July weather. Gooseberry bushes bending under their heavy load;

smooth gooseberries and hairy gooseberries, green, red, and yellow gooseberries, currants red, white, and black.   The hoary old bushes grow such fruit as you could rarely find in your orderly modern garden. This midsummer-time is Jane Faunthorpe's satur-nalia.   She 'spends the long warm afternoons in a dwarf forest of prickly shrubs, tears her frocks to absolute ribbons, neglects her stockings, lets her long tails of brown hair go loose and ragged as a beggar girl's, and in her sister's words makes an object of herself.   The fruit she eats all day, the lettuces and other green stuffs she consumes at supper-time, would lay an ordinary mortal low, under the deadly grip of cholera; but Jenny is none the worse for her intemperance, and rises with renewed vigour every morning to run riot among the gooseberry bushes.   Dr. Faunthorpe remonstrates occasionally on the subject of his youngest niece's unkempt and down-at-heel condition, and remarks plaintively that she is not exactly a credit to him or to her sisters.   But Marion flings the burden of blame on Jane.   She is quite incorrigible.   It is useless to attempt improvement.

'If I were to work my fingers to the bone to-day, she'd be just as ragged to-morrow,' argues Marion.

'But, my love, there are rents, absolute rents in her frock which might surely be sewn up with very little labour,' pleads the mild doctor.

'Then let her sew them up herself,' exclaims Marion, 'she's old enough. I shan't encourage her to be a tear-coat by doing all her mending.'

The old servant and factotum, Hester, girds at both,—Jenny for her sluttishness, Marion for her fine-ladyism.

'You can pore your eyes out over a bit of trumpery to make yourself smart,' she says to the elder damsel, 'yet you won't thread a needle to make your sister tidy.'

Thus Jenny is an element of discord in the house, and, conscious of this fact, confines herself but seldom within its walls. She rambles about the garden, or squats in dusty corners, or hides among the gooseberry bushes all day long. She has sundry members of the animal kingdom for her amusement, a blind jackdaw in a dilapidated old cage in the stable, caterpillars and green beetles in paper boxes or old pickle bottles, a family of white mice, a hutch full of rabbits. With these companions she is perfectly happy.

Sibyl finds her youngest sister sitting on the ground in a spot where the gooseberries grow thickest, sunburnt, disorderly, her plentiful brown hair hanging loosely over her shoulders, no collar, no cuffs, a dirty holland gown out at elbows and too short at the wrists, and two stout legs stretched straight before her in wrinkled stockings, two over-grown feet in clumsy boots making themselves ungracefully conspicuous. Jenny Faunthorpe is not a bad-looking girl, and may possibly develop even-. tually into a good-looking woman, but in her present wild state she has not that air of refinement which Sibyl would like to see in her sister.

To-day, however, Sibyl is anxious to be on good terms with this young Bohemian.

' Well, child, burning yourself to a cinder as usual,' she begins, ' and you might have such a nice complexion if you would only take care of it.'

' I should never have *your* complexion,' answers

the reprobate child without looking up; 'I'm not made of tinted marble, like Mr. Somebody's coloured Venus.'

'Get up, you silly girl, and let me have a look at you.'

'De-ah me!' cries Jenny, 'So you know me to-day; you didn't seem to recognise me on the racecourse last week, in uncle Robert's pony chaise You needn't have been so proud. We were carriage people just as much as you. A carriage is a carriage anyhow.'

'There are some carriages that are a great deal more disgraceful than walking,' exclaims Sibyl, forgetting the necessity of conciliating this out-spoken child.

'Yes, carriages that people ride in through lick spittling, and turning their backs on their truest benefactors,' cries the incorrigible Jane. 'If it hadn't been for uncle Robert's goodness we might all have died of starvation when we were tiny children. Uncle Trenchard did not think of us then, oh dear no. But uncle Trenchard can leave us a lot of money, and uncle Robert can't, so we

court uncle Trenchard. At least some of us
do—not a hundred miles from this gooseberry
bush.'

'Well, Jenny, I came here this overpowering
afternoon, through that baking town, on purpose to
see you, but as you're not particularly civil I may as
well go back.'

'No, you needn't,' cries Jenny, springing up from
the ground and letting a shower of gooseberry skins
fall from her lap. 'I feel better tempered now that
I've given you a piece of my mind, but when you
see me again in a public place, Sib, don't you try to
cut me, because it won't do. I'm not going to be
cut by my own flesh and blood. I'll run and coax
Hester to let us have tea in the arbour. You
know that old vine in the corner; it doesn't grow
grapes, but it grows lots of leaves; me and Tom
Sprig have made an arbour, and trained that old vine
over it.'

'I should say Tom Sprig and I.'

'Should you? I shouldn't. If I'm not of more
consequence than a boy that comes to litter the
pony for eighteen-pence a week, I don't know

English grammar. Such an awfully jolly arbour, Sib. I'll run and see about tea.'

There is a vision of legs whirling wildly down the garden walk, and Jane is gone to hold parley with honest old Hester, who stands at a wash-tub by the back kitchen window, the perspiration pouring down her toilworn face. There are women in the world who bear all the burden of family cares without the sweets of kindred, and this faithful old servant is one of these. She has toiled and striven for Dr. Faunthorpe's nieces as if they were her own flesh and blood; has scolded and praised them, worked for them and thought for them, risen early and gone to bed late; and except that she is recognised in a general way as a good creature, too fond of using her tongue, she has not much reward for her labours in this sublunary sphere.

'Tea in the arbour!' cries her shrill voice, 'and on a washing day! Who ever heard of such a thing? You're never happy unless you're giving trouble.'

'But we must have tea somewhere, musn't we, stupid? And what's the difference of our having it in the arbour if I carry out the tray?'

'Yes, and smash half the cups and saucers.'

'Oh dear yes; I'm always smashing things, ain't
I? Who was it broke the pie-dish yesterday? Not
me.'

The damsel opens a cupboard, takes out loaf and
butter-dish, whisks a tea-tray from its shelf, and
arranges cups and saucers with a tremendous clatter, while the longsuffering Hester is wiping her
shrivelled hands. There is a good deal of squab-
bling, but the tray is laid between the disputants,
the tea made, a plateful of bread and butter, and
another plate of plain currant cake cut, and Hester
bears the tray off to the garden, Jenny following
with the cake and bread and butter, radiant at her
victory.

The arbour, in an angle of the crumbling red
brick wall, is not altogether a bad place after its
fashion. An ancient fig tree, which grows anyhow,
and bears innumerable figs that never ripen, shields
it on one side, the vine covers the other side, and
trails over the top. Tom Sprig, the stable-boy, has
exercised his mechanical genius in constructing a
rude table and bench out of old packing cases—

Jenny has painted bench and table a vivid green.

Here Hester places the tea-tray, under protest, after a passing nod—not a very friendly salutation—to Sibyl.

'If you like earwigs in your teas you'll have 'em in plenty,' she says, as she surveys the rustic banquet. 'There's no accounting for tastes;' and with this remark she returns to her wash-tub.

'I'll run and fetch Marion,' says Jenny.

'Not just this minute, dear,' says Sibyl, stopping her. 'I want to have a few words with you alone.'

For an instant or so Jenny apprehends a lecture, but as Sibyl winds her arm caressingly round her sister's waist, Jenny opines that she is wanted to share some agreeable confidence.

'You are going to tell me about *him*,' she cries eagerly. 'Do, Sib. When is it to be?'

'Whom do you mean by *him*?'

'Sir Wilford Cardonnel, of course. Anybody could see that it was a case of smite.'

'Jenny, what horrid language!'

'I mean to say that he was smitten. And he

has called on you with Mrs. Stormont, too. That
must mean something.'

'Who told you that?'

'Hester knows a young woman that's housemaid
at Mrs. Stormont's, and she tells us all that goes on
Above Bar. Oh, we're not quite cut off from the
world of fashion, though we do live at the shabby
end of the town. When is it to be, Sib?'

They are walking slowly up and down the path
by the old red wall, and the border where clove
carnations and cabbage roses grow in wildest luxuri-
ance.

'When is *what* to be, child?'

'Your wedding. When are you going to be
Lady Cardonnel? You'll let me be bridesmaid,
won't you, Sib? I'll try to be graceful. I'll take
such pains with myself for a month beforehand, and
I'm your own sister, you know. It stands to reason
I ought to be bridesmaid; I've just as good a right
as Marion. When is it going to be, Sib?'

'Never,' cries Sibyl, turning upon her angrily;
'and if you allow your tongue to run on in this
ridiculous manner I shan't come to see you any more.'

'But you'd marry him if he asked you, sure to goodness,' exclaims Jane. 'Sure to goodness' is a favourite ejaculation of Hester's.

'No, I should not, Jenny;' and, in a gush of feeling or remorse, or utter helplessness, Sibyl flings her arms round Jane Faunthorpe's neck, and sobs upon her shoulder.

'Sibyl, whatever *is* the matter?'

'I'll tell you presently. Oh, Jenny, I'm very miserable.'

'Miserable, with that lovely hat, and with all that Madeira work on your dress?'

'Yes, Jane. I want some one to help me, some one to pity me, and I would rather trust you than Marion.'

'Trust me, then. You might trust me with high treason,' cries Jenny, vehemently, her notions of history being for the most part derived from Mr. Ainsworth's novels. 'If I had my flesh torn off with red-hot pincers, or my feet screwed up in iron boots, I wouldn't tell. You'd get no Rye House Plot out of me.'

'Yes, I think I can trust you, Jenny,' says

Sibyl, drying her tears. 'You were always my favourite sister, you know.'

'I didn't know it, though I remember you said so when I told you about that man.'

'Yes, dear, I always loved you best.'

'I'm very glad to hear it, Sib ; and I shall be your bridesmaid, sha'n't I, when you marry, and wear white muslin over white silk, a pink sash, and a wreath of pink daisies ? That's *my* idea of a bridesmaid's dress.'

'I shall never have any bridesmaids, Jenny.'

'WHAT do you mean by not having any brides-maids, Sibyl?' demands Jenny, as the sisters walk slowly along the garden path. 'You can't be married without them, can you?'

'Yes,' answers Sibyl; 'I know a girl who was married one morning with not a soul belonging to her in the church.'

'Gracious goodness! Who gave her away?'

'The beadle.'

'How horrid!'

'And now let's be serious, Jenny. Do you remember that man who came here two years ago in the winter, and questioned you about me?'

'As if I were likely to forget him!'

'If he were to come again, and want to see me, what should you say to him?'

'Well, that would depend upon how he was dressed. If he looked like a beggar, as he did last time, I should tell him some bouncer or other, and send him away, because I'm sure you wouldn't like a ragged person to come and ask for you at Lancaster Lodge.'

'What a sensible girl you are, Jenny!'

'Yes, I believe my head is screwed on pretty tight.'

'Now listen, darling. If that poor young man should come here again and ask you questions about me, you must contrive to send him away with the idea that I am ever so far from Redcastle. In Scotland, Ireland, anywhere you like. But you must not say that I am abroad, as he knows that I'm within a twenty-four hours' post of London. Say what you like, but don't let him know that I'm in Redcastle; and whatever you do, don't mention uncle Trenchard's name.'

'I'll be as secret as the grave,' answers Jane, solemnly. 'Don't you think that tea will be overdrawn?'

'Let it draw a little longer. We all like it strong, you know. You shall have this hat next week, Jenny, since you think it pretty.'

' Pretty! It's absolutely divine! Marion will be awfully jealous.'

' I can't help that. If Marion were a little more civil I should give her plenty of pretty things. Now listen, Jenny. Suppose that poor young man were to say curious things—were to tell you something strange about me——'

' What could he tell me?' asks Jane, making her eyes as round as marbles.

' Never mind what. You must not be surprised, and you must not let him discover anything from your manner. Above all, remember that he is to know nothing about uncle Trenchard. It is nothing wrong that I am asking you to do, Jenny, except so far as it is wrong to tell a falsehood, and I really think even that is excusable when one is in a great dilemma.'

'I don't mind telling a bouncer,' says Jane, boldly. ' Bouncers never weigh much on my conscience.'

' It is very wicked to tell stories in a general way. You ought to know that, Jenny. But this is quite an exceptional case. It is all for the best. All will come right in the end. And I shall love you dearly, Jenny, if you will help me out of my difficulties. Mind, the person I speak of may not come here again. I only wish you to be prepared for him if he should come.'

'I'm prepared,' answered Jenny, boldly. 'Poor fellow! I did feel sorry for him that bitter winter day. He looked so tired and worn—very good-looking, too, in spite of all. How handsome he must be when he's well dressed!'

'Yes, he is very handsome,' says Sibyl, pensively.

'And you like him, Sib—just a little bit?'

'I loved him with all my heart—I love him still —I am true to him through all difficulties. Remember that always, Jenny.'

'Gracious!' cries Jenny. 'And it is on his account that you would refuse to marry Sir Wilford Cardonnel if he were to ask you?'

'Yes, Jenny.'

'But I say, Sib, suppose he should come to the front door, and Marion or Hester should get hold of him?'

'You must be on the watch to prevent that. If he comes at all, he is likely to come within the next few days. I rely upon your cleverness to prevent his seeing Marion or Hester.'

' Very well. It will be difficult, but I'll do my best. And now I'd better run and call Marion to tea, or she'll begin to think there are secrets between you and I.'

' Between you and me, Jenny!'

' Oh, bother! If I say me, it's I; if I say I, it's me. I'll run for Marion.'

Again appears that vision of legs whirling wildly, and scanty skirts flying in the wind. Sibyl strolls along the path, and looks at the big cabbage roses, the red crinkled wall, the sprawling vegetable marrows, the flush of uncultivated fertility. Red and yellow dragon's-mouth flourishes on the wall. Stonecrop in full flower yonder on the sloping roof of the tumbledown old shed, that serves as a stable, converts the thatch into a roof of gold. Butterflies, bees, and all the summer insects, are flying from flower to flower, carrying the yellow pollen on their honey-smeared wings, and intermarrying all the families of blossoms as they flutter to and fro. It is only poverty's poorly tended garden, but how full of colour and perfume and beauty! It is almost as good as uncle Trenchard's velvet lawn and mosaic flower-beds. 'One feels more at home here,' thinks Sibyl.

'I wish I were Jenny or Marion, without a care for what to-morrow may bring forth,' she thinks; 'even though I forfeited my chance of uncle Trenchard's fortune.'

Marion comes along the path by the gooseberry bushes presently, tearing her muslin skirt once or twice by contact with the straggling thorny branches on the way, and muttering little ejaculations which come as near swearing as a lady can permit herself to venture.

'Plague take the brambles!' she cries. 'At uncle Trenchard's the kitchen-garden is in its proper place, not all mixed up with the flowers. How you must laugh at us, Sibyl, for drinking tea in such an arbour as that, and calling it pleasure!'

'Not at all. I am very fond of uncle Robert's old garden; and I think everything grows here better than at Lancaster Lodge.'

'It's very considerate of you to say that, in order to reconcile us to our lowly lot,' replies Marion, with a sneer, as she **takes her** place on the narrow green bench, and begins **to pour** out the **tea**.

'Milk and **sugar, I suppose? You used to take both** when I had **the privilege of being** intimate with you—of course **it's cream at Lancaster Lodge— and the sugar doesn't look as if it had the** jaundice, as ours does.'

Marion is **not** comfortably **awake yet; her eyes have a watery look;** the **great lump** of hair **and** padding with **which she adorns the top** of her head **is pushed awry; her toilet has an air of faded fashion, of tumbled** frippery, which is suggestive **of a struggle to be** fine under disadvantages. No **dress is more becoming to a girlish wearer than fresh** uncreased **muslin**; but **a muslin** dress that has been worn three **days and** slept **in three** afternoons **is not the loveliest of garments.** Marion has pinned a bow here and **there, and** has put on the last fashionable ruffle **at one and** elevenpence threefarthings, and has done her best to embellish the soiled muslin, but the result is failure, and **she** feels that it **is so as she looks at** Sibyl's pure white cambric and delicate Madeira embroidery.

' I wonder you are so fond of mauve, Sibyl,' she says, after a critical survey of her sister's hat. ' It doesn't suit you by any means. You look as white as chalk.'

' The warm weather is rather trying,' answers Sibyl.

' And you have such black marks under your eyes.'

' I have not slept well lately.'

' You look like it. One would think you had something dreadful on your conscience. Take that horrid caterpillar off the bread-and-butter plate, Jenny. I declare this den of yours swarms with reptiles. I saw a toad under the bench yesterday.'

' Toads are valuable animals,' answers Jane. ' They eat the snails like one o'clock.'

' Another of your ladylike similes. Poor uncle Robert! I pity him when I think how his money was wasted in paying for that child's schooling. The only education she got was the bad language she picked up in the street on her way to school and back. If uncle Trenchard had a spark of family feeling he'd send her to a good boarding-school, where she'd be licked into shape.'

'Licked into shape isn't *my* idea of elegant language,' remarks Jenny, with her mouth full of bread-and-butter.

'But I forgot,' pursues Marion, ignoring this interruption. 'Uncle Trenchard reserves all his generosity for *one* member of this family. Any attempt of ours to obtain a share of his favour would be regarded as an intrusion. We are outsiders. But if ever a child was going to ruin for want of proper tuition, Jenny is that child.'

'I should have thought you might have taught her yourself, Marion,' says Sibyl.

'Should you? Then perhaps you'll be kind enough to try the experiment some morning for an hour or two before you think any more about it. A more unteachable brat I never came across in all my life, and I took the fourth class at Miss Worrie's for a week when you were laid up with scarlatina.'

'I don't like to be taught by an ignoramus,' exclaims the contumacious Jenny. 'Who was it said *nous allerons* was the future of *aller*? People should learn before they teach. At least, that's my idea.'

Sibyl, wearied with these recriminatory passages,

looks at her watch, and finds that it is time for her
to go back to Lancaster Lodge.

'It's half an hour's walk,' she says. 'And I
must be dressed for dinner by seven, uncle Trenchard
likes me to be in the drawing-room half an hour
before dinner.'

'Ah, no wonder you don't care about our currant cake when you're going to have a regular tuck
out at half-past seven,' exclaims Jenny.

'If you knew how little appetite I have for
uncle Trenchard's grand dinners, Jenny, you wouldn't
envy me,' says Sibyl.

'In fact, my dear Jenny,' exclaims Marion, going
over to the enemy, 'Sibyl is a woman of fashion, a
superior being whom you and I are not qualified to
comprehend.'

This remark winds up the skirmish, Sibyl wishes
Marion good-bye, and leaves the arbour, followed by
Jenny, who hangs on her as they walk down the
narrow path. At the kitchen window Sibyl pauses
to say a civil word to Hester.

'And how are you, Hester, this warm weather?'
she inquires.

'Just as hard at work as if it was **cold weather**,' replies Hester, **in** no wise mollified by the sweetness **of** this address. '**Your uncle's shirts have to be** washed, even if it is the **dog** days, and **the** perspiration running down one's **face. As to how I am in** myself, I haven't got time to **think whether I'm ill** or well, and that's all about **it**.'

'I hope **uncle Robert** is feeling better **than when** I saw him last,' **remarks** Sibyl, playing with the ivory handle **of her parasol**, embarrassed by **the** faithful servant's stern **countenance**.

'Then he isn't,' snaps **Hester**. 'And a **deal you** care about it. I wouldn't be a n'ypocrite, if I was you, Miss Sibyl. You've got your rich uncle. Stick to him. **And** don't pretend **to care about the** poor uncle that **brought you up**.'

'Upon my word,' **exclaimed Sibyl, half** angry, '**I** wonder that **I** ever come here.'

'So do I, **miss. You come** so seldom that you might just as well stay away altogether. It would be more consistent.'

CHAPTER III.

AT half-past twelve o'clock on the following day Sibyl and Mr. Trenchard start on their drive to the How. It is more than an hour's drive, even with Mr. Trenchard's well-fed horses, who are used so little that they are in a chronic state of either wanting to run away or languishing into a crawl. Their paces between Redcastle and the How are an alternate bolt and dawdle, and perhaps, on the whole, they take more time about the journey than the less pampered steeds which ply for hire at Redcastle station.

Sir Wilford Cardonnel is smoking his cigar on the grassy walk inside the moat as Mr. Trenchard's carriage drives through the gateway. The How is a good old place of the moated grange order. Tudor gables and windows in front; roofs and chimneys at the back of the premises of an earlier period; a fine old chapel, which has been converted into a drawing-room; a monkish refectory, which has been made a billiard-room. The gardens are lovely, and that deep wide moat, with its dark still water and smooth green banks, adds not a little to their beauty. A swan comes sailing down the dark shining water as Sibyl alights, assisted by Sir Wilford, who has thrown away his cigar and come to welcome his guests.

'How late you are!' he exclaims. 'I have been expecting you for the last two hours. Now what will you see first?—the stables or the gardens?'

Sibyl is going to say the gardens, but Mr. Trenchard, who knows that his host's tastes are turfy, votes for the stables.

'I'm so glad you like stables,' exclaims Sir Wilford, addressing himself to Sibyl, as if the choice were hers. 'I'm rather proud of mine, you know. I've spent a good deal of money upon 'em. They were regular pigsties when I inherited the place. My poor father didn't care about his stables, you know. As long as he had a couple of carriage horses to drag the family about, a weight-carrying cob for his own use, and a pony or two for us

children, he was satisfied. His horses weren't members of his family. Why, in his time the gardeners
and farm labourers were as well accommodated as
the horses,' concludes Sir Wilford, as if this were
the summit of iniquity.

They traverse a shrubbery, and find themselves
in the stable department, a spacious quadrangle,
stone-paved, with a stone basin of water in the
middle. Numbered doors, and windows adorned
with flower-boxes, surround this neat square quadrangle, each door opening into a loose box, each
number belonging to a special quadruped in Sir
Wilford's stud. Within, the loose boxes are as neat
as a spinster annuitant's best parlour. Each horse is
provided with a cat or dog for company, while one
animal, more social than the rest, is not satisfied
without the society of a stable boy, who sits in a
corner of his box reading the paper all the summer
afternoon, while the lordly beast stares dreamily at
him across the swinging door, and makes an occasional snap at him, displaying an appalling range of
long yellow teeth, in pure playfulness.

Sibyl is introduced severally to the horses, who

are swathed in double sets of clothing, as if they were in Siberia.

'Why are the poor things wrapped up so this warm weather?' inquires Sibyl.

'That's to keep up the beauty of their coats, mum,' says a stable boy.

Numerous animals are unclothed, and brought out in the sunny quadrangle to display their various graces. They all seem pretty much alike to Sibyl, except that some are thin and some thick. Sibyl admires the slimmer animals, but Sir Wilford, Mr. Trenchard, and the stud groom go into raptures about the thicker and more stalwart quadrupeds.

'There's a shoulder!' says the groom, punching a bull-necked brute. 'Carry a church.'

'There are legs,' cries Sir Wilford, 'regular gate-posts!'

'Shall I bring out Bull of Bashan, sir?' inquires the stud groom, and another thick-set beast is led forth, plunging viciously to the rearwards as he emerges from his cool retreat.

Bull of Bashan is the gem of the stud. His leading qualification is cobbiness, thick neck, thick legs, a straight line from hock to fetlock, short barrel, broad chest, an eye like Jove to threaten or command, and not a white hair about him, as the stud groom remarks complacently. Time was when Bull of Bashan would have been esteemed a serviceable horse for a village miller, or a tenant farmer. To-day he is the last fashion for a gentleman of fortune.

'Ran away with a stable boy yesterday morning when he was being exercised,' says Sir Wilford, approvingly, patting the beast's solid shoulder, which familiarity the Bull resents by sticking his ears back till he appears to be unprovided with those appendages, and giving a vicious kick in the direction of his master's shins.

'How do you like the Bull, Miss Faunthorpe?'

'Isn't he rather bad tempered?' inquires Sibyl, doubtfully.

'Oh, he's a lively horse, I admit, but the best goer in the stable. The men don't care about riding him, but he and I understand each other,—don't we, Bull? There, take him in, Chanter.'

They look into other loose boxes, and Sibyl

begins to think there is no end to the horses; but the stable inspection is over at last, and they go back to the gardens, where the baronet's sisters condescend to join them.

Phœbe Cardonnel is a little more inclined to be civil to-day than she showed herself at Lancaster Lodge yesterday. She tells Sibyl the names of roses and ferns, and makes herself otherwise agreeable. This amelioration of the young lady's manners has been brought about by a domestic process which Sir Wilford calls 'a jolly good setting down.'

The baronet has informed his sisters in the plainest language that he considers Miss Faunthorpe the nicest girl he has met for a long time, that he has been informed that she has large expectations from the old Indian beggar, meaning Stephen Trenchard, and that in his, Sir Wilford's opinion, she would suit him admirably for a wife.

Whereupon the two sisters, Phœbe and Lavinia, as with one voice, exclaim in the words of Mrs. Stormont,—

'Wilford! a girl of no family.'

'Hang family!' ejaculates Sir Wilford. 'We've

got pedigree enough and to spare. The needful thing is ready money.

'Oh, Wilford, you are rich enough surely.'

'Oh, I can rub along, if that's what you mean,' answers the baronet. 'But I could buy the Longley Bottom Estate if I had fifty thousand to dispose of, and then I should be the largest landowner between this and York. There's an upland meadow that would make the finest gallop in England, and you know how badly I want some good training-ground.'

'Well, Wilford, if I were the head of the family I wouldn't degrade myself by a plebeian marriage for the sake of a few paltry thousands. You might have Lady Malvina Vielleroche for the asking.'

'But I never shall ask,' answers Sir Wilford decisively. 'Lady Malvina is a good deal too weedy for my money, and I don't like 'em that colour. I'd marry Miss Faunthorpe if she hadn't a sixpence, but of course I take all the more kindly to the notion on account of that old chap's cash. I shouldn't like to see Longley Manor owned by some three-quarter bred cockney.'

The result of this conversation, which took

place after dinner yesterday evening, is Phœbe Cardonnel's amiable welcome of to-day. She takes Sibyl up to her own room to take off her hat before luncheon, and Sibyl admires the fine old house with its spacious corridors, massive Tudor windows, and innumerable rooms. It is all so different from the formal splendour of Lancaster Lodge. Here all is picturesque, full of old associations, suggestive of ruffs and farthingales, silken hose, and jewelled sword-hilts. There must be a family ghost, of course, in such a house.

'It is a place whose mistress must feel like a queen,' thinks Sibyl, as she stands before the carved oak dressing-table, with its old Venice mirror, not quite so convenient as a modern dressing-table, but wondrous stately. From the wide mullioned window she sees the gardens and park spreading far away to the summer woods, and woods as well as park and gardens belong to Sir Wilford Cardonnel.

She can but think what a mighty conquest she has made, if Sir Wilford is really in love with her, as she can hardly doubt. She is just a little intoxicated by the idea. She feels as if she had been raised suddenly to a dizzy height, from which she must come toppling down presently. She feels as she has often felt in a dream years ago at Miss Worrie's boarding school, when her slumbers were frequently visited by a vision of pride in which she saw herself wooed by some rich and noble suitor, and from which she awoke at the shrill peal of the school-bell, to find herself in the bleak bare dormitory, with the prospect of a winter day's dreary toil before her.

Luncheon at the How is a bounteous and hospitable meal, in an oak paneled dining-room After luncheon they explore the old house, which although not a show place, is well worthy that honour. They look at the family pictures, which seem to Sibyl rather a collection of wigs than of faces, so much more distinctive are the wigs than the countenances they embellish. The portrait gallery is, of course, a compendium of the family history, and Sibyl here discovers that the Cardonnels have produced alternate commanders by land and sea, for the protection of their country, and have occasionally blossomed into a judge.

Stephen Trenchard takes his part in the day's proceedings with supreme patience; admires the family portraits just as he admired Sir Wilford's horses; and makes himself generally agreeable. It is only when he is seated in the carriage with his niece that the tension of the bow is relaxed, and weariness overshadows the Anglo-Indian's sallow countenance.

'Rather a long morning, Sibyl,' he says, 'and more sight-seeing than I care about; but I have borne it all for your sake. It will be a proud day for me if I live to see you mistress of that place. Yes, my dear, one of the proudest days of my life; and yet I have made many a conquest over fortune since I left Redcastle, more than fifty years ago, a gaunt hungry lad—turned my back resolutely on my native town, knowing very well that there was nothing but starvation for me if I stayed there any longer.'

Sibyl is silent. It would be cruel to dispel a fancy which evidently gives the old man plea-

sure. Let him dream on. If what Mrs. Stormont
says is true—and Stephen Trenchard's strength
is dwindling fast,—the end may come before he
is awakened from his dream.

'And it will please him better to leave me
his money if he thinks that I am going to be a
rich baronet's wife,' reasons Sibyl within herself.
'To add riches to riches is the delight of such
men.'

CHAPTER IV

JENNY'S VISITOR.

ANOTHER blazing July afternoon, and all the corn-fields baking under the ripening sunshine. Jenny Faunthorpe lolls in her favourite arm-chair—a dreadfully dilapidated arm-chair it is, with a faded chintz cover which is always grimy—in the surgery window. She is very fond of sitting in the surgery, chiefly because it is against her uncle's household laws—if any man so easy-going and mild as Dr. Faunthorpe can be said to be a law-giver in his household—that she should sit there. It is not an attractive apartment. It is dirtier than any other room in the house, Hester being strictly forbidden to interfere with things in this sacred chamber, or, in other words, to sweep, dust, or scour. Its atmosphere is odoriferous with compound rhubarb pills, colocynth, and pounded aloes. Its counter is sticky with the traces of divers medicines which have been compounded upon it.

But there are attractions for Jenny in the room notwithstanding, and she infinitely prefers it to the family parlour. There is the syrup of poppies yonder on the second shelf from the top, in the dusty recess where the spiders have such a good time of it, and Jenny often indulges herself with a few sips of that soporific decoction. If she has a surreptitious novel in her possession she hides it on one of the lower shelves, behind the delf jar of leeches, perhaps. Sometimes she takes the leeches out and plays with them. At other times, when she is quite sure of not being disturbed by Dr. Faunthorpe, she amuses herself by taking down sundry bottles and making up prescriptions of her own. Thus :—

> Syrup poppies, 1 oz.
>
> Honey, lots.
>
> Cons. roses, $\frac{1}{2}$ oz.
>
> Peppermint, 1 drachm.
>
> Tamarinds, 2 oz.
>
> Aqua pura, 4 oz.

This afternoon, however, she has a particular reason for preferring the surgery to her usual happy hunting-grounds **among** the gooseberry bushes. **Faithful to her** promise **to** Sibyl, she makes the surgery window **her post** of observation, so that **if the young man** she expects should approach by the front door she may be ready to receive him, and cut off all communication with Hester. Should he **come to** the garden wall, **on** the other **hand, as on his** previous visit, there **can be no harm** done, **as the wall** adjoining **the lane is** beyond Hester's ken. With infinite diplomacy **Jenny has contrived to get** Marion out of the way for **the whole** day **by** persuading her to take the train to Krampston and visit **her old** schoolfellow, **Maria Harrison, the** Krampston Wesleyan minister's daughter, **with whom Marion has** kept **up some** semblance **of** friendship, **although the tastes of the two young** ladies are **widely at variance, Miss** Harrison being, as becomes **her, of a serious turn of** mind, while Marion is to **the** last degree frivolous. If there is one thing which Marion enjoys more **than** another in Maria's society it is the opportunity which it gives her to talk over Sibyl, whose goings on, gay **apparel, and** chariots **and** horses, Miss Harrison

contemplates with the disapproving eye of the
Hebrew prophets. Jeremiah himself did not de-
nounce the foolish daughters of Israel with more
vigour than Miss Harrison exhibits towards her old
schoolfellow.

Thus it is that whenever Marion is particularly
offended with Sibyl she is always in the humour for
a visit to Miss Harrison, whose home, though
unpretentious in its character, and situated in an
obscure by way of the busy port of Krampston, is
comfortable in its arrangements, and of a hospitable
turn. The five o'clock tea at the minister's table is
a plentiful and substantial meal, which makes an
excellent substitute for dinner, and renders supper a
superfluity.

Jenny, turning to account this idiosyncrasy of
her elder sister's, has persuaded Marion that she
owes Miss Harrison a visit, and that to-day is a good
opportunity for the settlement of that debt. Marion
has allowed herself to be persuaded, has put on her
best bonnet, and departed for Krampston in the one
o'clock train, meaning to have a good look at the
shops, which means a two hours' perambulation of

the principal streets, before proceeding to Miss Harrison's paternal dwelling.

'You needn't expect me till you see me,' says Marion at departing. 'For if there's an evening service at Little Bethel I shall be obliged to go, though if there are two people in the Scriptures I dislike more than another it's Ahab and Jezebel, and they always crop up in Mr. Harrison's sermons.'

Jenny has thus made the coast clear. It is Hester's day for cleaning the kitchen and out-houses, a day upon which the Miss Faunthorpes must either open the door to patient or casual visitor, or encounter Hester's wrath, that faithful servant having a temper which is aggravated by hearth-stoning difficult corners and awkward steps, and exasperated to fever point by scrubbing worm-eaten old floors, which 'never do one no credit.'

Jenny is quite sure that Hester will not appear till she brings in the tea-tray, scarlet of visage and perspiring, and puts it on the table with a bang and a clatter, exclaiming, 'There now, you've got your tea, and don't come worrying for anything else.'

It is between three and four—the sleepiest hour

in the slumberous balmy day, and Jenny basks in
the sunshiny surgery window, with folded arms,
watching the wasps and vagabond bees bouncing
their stupid heads against the roses in the dusty
front garden.   It is the very hour in which Sibyl and
Mr. Trenchard are returning from the How, and the
first day of Jenny's watch.

Just as the old minster clock with its mellow
tongue chimes the half-hour a dusty wayfarer comes
in sight, and Jenny cries out loud,—

'It's the very man, by all that's wonderful! but
dressed like a gentleman this time; and oh, how
nice he looks!'

Yes, it is the man she saw in the lane two
winters ago, tired, footsore, out at elbows.   To-day
he is as well clad as any man in Redcastle, and he
walks as if he had only come from the station.

He looks about him doubtfully for a minute or
so, as if unfamiliar with the front of Dr. Faunthorpe's
house, then sees the name upon the brass plate,
and approaches boldly, opens the gate, and comes in.

'If Marion or Hester were in the way now it
would be all UP,' Jenny says to herself.

Before the stranger can ring she has opened the door, and stands face to face with him upon the threshold.

'You're the very person I wanted to see,' exclaims Alexis Secretan as Jenny confronts him, her big round eyes staring their hardest; 'I'm lucky in finding you in the way.'

'Luckier than you know of,' thinks Jenny. 'Are you a patient ?' she demands aloud. 'If you are, uncle's out, and you can't have any medicine till after seven o'clock. Between seven and nine in the evening are his hours, or before nine in the morning.'

'Nonsense, child ! You must remember me, surely.'

Jane Faunthorpe's face expresses a total blankness. She shakes her head stolidly.

'Perhaps I look a little more decent to-day than I did one winter afternoon two years and a half ago,' says Alexis, with a laugh, 'but I'm the man who spoke to you across the garden wall. Do you remember now ? '

'I have a faint recollection,' replies Jenny, with a languid *hauteur*, which is very fairly imitated from

Sibyl. 'Come into the surgery, young man, if you please.'

Alexis laughs at the mode of address, and follows her down a step into that temple of the healing art.

Jenny enjoys the situation, and means to make the most of it. She looks at the stranger critically, as he drops into one of the frayed horsehair chairs, where parish patients are accustomed to sit awaiting Dr. Faunthorpe's opinion as the fiat of fate—the opinion rarely going beyond the statement that the patient is not so well as he might be, and that his condition will be improved by the medicine which Dr. Faunthorpe is about to give him. If, after this, the patient goes home and dies, it is his look-out. The parish has done all it can for him.

'I want to know all about your sister Sibyl,' says Alexis, looking round the shabby room, and thinking that this home of his wife's uncle's is not much better than Mrs. Bonny's one pair front in Dixon Street, Chelsea. 'Is she at home?'

Jane shakes her head dolefully, and heaves a sigh which would do credit to an actress of transpontine melodrama.

'I was in hopes you had come to tell us something about her,' she says, 'for it's a hard thing to have one's eldest sister wandering about the world no one knows where.'

'You mean to tell me that you don't know where she is at this present time!' exclaims Alexis.

'That's precisely the fact. She was governessing in Jersey when we heard from her last, but that's full ten months ago, and she's too much of a rolling stone to have stayed as long as that in one place. Especially as she told us that the lady had red hair and used to fly into passions,' adds Jenny, with a graphic touch that she thinks will give reality to her narrative.

'What was the lady's name?'

'Mrs. Yokohama Gray,' says Jenny on the spur of the moment, reminiscent of the advertisement of a certain dress fabric which she has perused with keenest interest.

'Yokohama,' repeats Alexis, 'that's rather a queer surname.'

'Well, it was very *like* that, if not that exactly.'

'Jersey,' says Alexis, thoughtfully, 'when last

you heard of your sister she was in Jersey, and that was ten months ago?'

Jenny counts her fingers meditatively, and appears to enter upon an abstruse calculation.

'Exactly ten months,' she answers finally.

'Could you show me your sister's letter?'

'It's torn up. Uncle Robert never keeps his letters.'

'But is not Dr. Faunthorpe anxious about your sister? It seems such a strange thing for him to be ignorant of her fate.'

'Of course it is. But Sibyl's a strange girl. Uncle Robert has had many a sleepless night on her account. I dare say we shall get a letter from her some day, telling us that she has gone with a lady to Peru, or Kamstchatka, or some of those hot climates where mosquitoes devour you all night, and alligators hide themselves under your bolster.'

Alexis sighs wearily.

'I should like to see your uncle,' he says, 'he might tell me more.'

'Not a bit of it,' replies Jenny, who has posed herself gracefully on a corner of the surgery table and swings her leg to and fro, **as if** rather admiring the shabby leather boot **at the end** of it, deficient of **every alternate** button. 'Uncle Robert couldn't tell you a word more than I've told you. **In** fact, he **mightn't** tell you quite as much.'

'**It's** hard to be left in **the dark like this**,' says Alexis.

. ' It's hard upon us, but **I** can't **see that it matters much to you**," remarks **Jenny**. 'If you are ever so deeply in love with Sibyl, she isn't so **much to you as she to us**.'

'Isn't **she ?**' exclaims Alexis. 'Suppose **I tell** you that she is more **to me** than **she is to any one else** in the world, **and that** I am determined not to be **kept in ignorance of her present position**. She **is my** wife, Miss Faunthorpe, **and the law of** the land, as well **as the law of God** which preceded that law, gives a husband **custody** of his **wife**.'

'Gracious goodness !' ejaculates Jenny, slipping off **the angle of** the **table, and** recovering her equilibrium **with a struggle**, 'do you mean that my sister Sibyl is **a married** woman ?'

'**She is my** wife. **An unfaithful wife,** for she

deserted me because I was poor. Yet I am weak enough to love her still, and I will go to the end of the world to find her.'

'My!' exclaims Jenny. 'This is the awfullest thing I ever heard of.'

'You can understand therefore that I have some right to make inquiries about your sister, and that I am justified in insisting upon seeing your uncle Robert.'

'Oh, but you mustn't,' cries Jenny, with overwhelming energy. 'You mustn't breathe one syllable about your marriage to uncle Robert. It would be the ruin of all of us if you did. Don't you know that we are no better than paupers dependent upon his charity? He'd turn Marion and me out of doors if he knew that Sibyl had married without his consent. You don't know what a man he is. Onr innocence wouldn't help us. He'd wash his hands of the whole lot of us.'

'That would be a very vindictive course of action.'

'Uncle Robert is vindictive,' exclaims Jenny. 'He doesn't know what it is to forgive. Do you

suppose he'd ever get over Sibyl's ingratitude ? **He**
never would, and he'd **wreak his** vengeance upon
unoffending **Marion and still more** unoffending me,
for I'm not old enough to go and get married
clandestinely, **if I wanted to.'**

'**I had no idea your uncle was such a**
Tartar.'

'**Sibyl** ought to have told you. **I thought
when a person married a person they always**
described their **relations** to that **person.'**

'**I had an impression that** Dr. Faunthorpe
was quite **an** easy-going little **man,'** says Alexis.

'Ah, Sibyl may have felt it her duty to **make**
the best of **him.** You see he gives us **the bread**
we eat, and **one** ought to be thankful for **one's**
daily bread **even** if it's **two days old, and** scrapy
as to butter. **We don't ask** for **butter in our**
prayers, you see.'

'And you expect me to leave this place without making any further inquiries about my wife ?'
demands Alexis.

'What's **the** use of inquiring when you've had
all the information any one can give you **here ?'**

asks Jane, with a practical air. 'You'd much better go to Jersey and inquire there.'

'Yet you say Sibyl is likely to have left Jersey by this time.'

'More than likely. She was always fond of change. She may have gone to Calcutta, or St. Petersburg, or Hong-Kong, or Scarborough, or anywhere where governesses are wanted. But you might trace her *from* Jersey, you know. It would be a good starting-point.'

'You tell me that she has never been home since she first left this place to go to Mrs. Hazleton.'

'Never,' says Jenny, so resolutely that Alexis ought to know she is telling a falsehood.

'Well, if I can do myself no good by seeing your uncle——'

'And are sure to do us a lot of harm,' interjects Jenny.

'I may as well go away without seeing him, and trust to my own wits for finding your sister.'

'Decidedly,' replies Jenny. 'A clever young man like you can't be long at a loss.'

'Good-bye, Miss Faunthorpe.'

'You'd better call me Jenny, if you're my brother-in-law.'

'Good-bye, Jenny; thou hast comforted me marvellous much. I must go and try my luck elsewhere.'

'If there was anything in this way I could do for you,' says Jenny, waving her hand in the direction of the shelves, 'the surgery is at your service. I know the bottles as well as uncle does. Anything from syrup of squills to corrosive supplement. Uncle sends a good deal of that to his parish patients, and I believe it cures them, but I'm not quite sure whether they take it externally or internally.'

'There's one little blue bottle up there that might be useful to me,' says Alexis, with a touch of bitterness.

He points to a dark blue bottle that stands in a corner by itself on the topmost shelf in a recess by the fireplace, and away from the light. A bottle with a gilt label.

'Gracious!' cries Jenny. 'That's prussic acid —deadly poison.'

'A short cut out of a man's troubles, Jenny. But I suppose a man who takes that way is something of a poltroon, and I'm not disposed to try it yet awhile.   Good-bye, Jenny.'

'Good-bye, brother-in-law.   I'm really very sorry for you, and I hope things will come right in the end.   You may kiss me if you like, as we are such near relatives.'

Thus privileged, Alexis imprints a brotherly kiss upon Jane's forehead, and with a final sigh of disappointment departs.

CHAPTER V.

BAFFLED where he had expected to succeed, **Alexis Secretan** is at a loss what to do next. No doubt of Jenny's truthfulness presents itself to his mind. youthful candour beamed in that open countenance of hers. How could he imagine the craft of the serpent in a child who seemed simple as the sucking dove?

What is he to do? Go to Jersey and hunt for Mrs. Yokohama Gray on the chance of finding Sibyl still with that lady, despite Jenny's assertion of her sister's fickleness? This seems the most obvious course for him to take, and he loses no time in taking it. The journey from Redcastle in Yorkshire to the Channel Islands is a long one, and it is only on the third day after his interview with Jane Faunthorpe that Alexis finds himself at St. Heliers.

Vain are his inquiries for Mrs. Yokohama Gray, or for any Mrs. Gray with a name approaching Yokohama in sound. He finds a Mrs. Gray pure and simple, but she is a laundress, and certainly not in a position to afford the luxury of a governess for her children. Alexis pursues his inquiry in every quarter likely to afford information. He sees postmasters, lodging-house keepers, librarians, and tries to obtain tidings of any lady with a pretty governess residing in the Island. Sibyl might be remembered for her pretty face, he thinks, where her name was unknown or forgotten.

All his efforts are vain. He starts upon various false scents, wastes a great deal of time and trouble, and leaves the island at last, thoroughly dispirited.

What more is there for him to do? Nothing assuredly, unless he can extort the secret of his wife's whereabouts from that inflexible young woman, Jane Dimond. It seems such a hard thing to have Sibyl's letter in his pocket, to know that she is within a day's post, and yet not be able to find her. At Southampton, while he is loitering

about waiting for the train that is to take him
back to London, he remembers that he has or ought
to have a kinswoman living in the neighbourhood
of Winchester. A maiden lady, his father's first
cousin, has lived all her life on a small estate near
that cathedral city. He remembers spending a
month at Cheswold Grange with his father and
mother during one of those rare visits which they
made to their native country. He was a child at
this time, and it had struck him since that his
father must have had some stronger motive than
family affection in coming over to England to
visit a quiet maiden lady, living in an out-of-the-
way village.

His father had possibly some idea of securing
Miss Secretan's fortune for himself or his boy.
Philip Secretan was assuredly the last of men to
degrade himself by courting a wealthy relative, but
he may have thought it his duty to his boy to keep
on friendly terms with the owner of the only estate
remaining to the family.

As years went on Mr. Secretan had grown
more indolent in his habits, and less inclined to

cross the channel, but one of his farewell injunctions
to Alexis when the young man last visited him
had reference to Matilda Secretan.

'Go and spend a few days with your cousin
Matilda now and then, Alex,' said the father. 'She
was very fond of you when you were a little boy,
and I know she'll be pleased to see you now you've
grown into a fine young man. It's a quiet, out-of-
the-way place for you to visit, but you will be made
much of by the old lady, and I dare say you can get
a little shooting there in October. Lord Starborough's preserves are close by, and your cousin
was always on good terms with her neighbours.'

Alexis promised most dutifully, and was always
intending to perform ; but the visit to Miss Secretan
was a business so easy to accomplish that it was
deferred indefinitely. Alexis thought it would be
a pity to go earlier than October, on account of
Lord Starborough's pheasants, and three Octobers
came and went without his finding leisure for the
visit. Then came the sale of his commission, and
he felt he should hardly like to face his cousin
Matilda under such awkward circumstances. He

would have to explain things, and he hated explanations. Next came his entanglement in Cupid's fatal net, and he had not a spare thought for Miss Secretan. Then followed his marriage and rapid descent in the social scale. He had sore need of a friend in those days; but as he had neglected his cousin Matilda in his brief day of prosperity, he could not approach her in his destitution. He might stoop to ask a favour of aunt Gorsuch, at whose house he had been a familiar guest, but he could not beg of Miss Secretan, to whom he was a stranger. He had a faint recollection of her as an old lady with silvery hair in corkscrew curls, a high nose, delicate peach-bloom cheeks, a slim straight figure, and a dress of rich black silk, like a clergyman's presentation gown. That she had been very kind to him, and that his life had been made particularly pleasant to him at Cheswold Grange, he could remember distinctly. He remembered telling Sibyl about his rich maiden cousin, as they sat by the fire in Dixon Street one November evening, building castles in a brief interval of hopefulness. He had described that childish visit to Cheswold, and his girl-wife had been fascinated by his picture of the pretty English country house and gardens, the meadows, and the trout-stream in which he had made his juvenile attempts at fly-fishing.

'Why shouldn't your cousin leave you her estate, Alex?' Sibyl had said eagerly. 'Wouldn't that be a happy thing?'

'A very happy thing, love, but not a likely turn of the wheel by any means,' he had answered. 'I have never seen my cousin since I was ten years old. Whatever chances I had in that direction have been forfeited by my neglect.'

'Upon my word, Alexis, you seem to have delighted in throwing away fortune,' Sibyl had answered, with a touch of anger. And after that she had given way to low spirits for the rest of the evening, and had talked of Cheswold Grange as a property that must have come to her husband if he had not wilfully flung away his prospect of inheritance.

To-day Alexis, sorely perplexed which way to turn in the maze of life, is inclined to dwell upon the memory of his boyish pleasures at Cheswold. He is so near the quiet old place, within twenty miles at most. **Why should he not go and see** Matilda Secretan ? **He** can approach her without degradation now that he **is a** prosperous, money-earning man. He has no thought of that possible inheritance. **It** is not in his nature to calculate upon **a** thing of that kind ; **but,** being so utterly alone in **the world just now, he feels that** it would do him good to grasp the hand of a relative—to receive kindness **and** sympathy **from one who had known** his father and mother.

The train that was to have carried him to London conveys **him to** Winchester. At the station he **is told that Cheswold is three miles from** the city, so **he determines to** walk **the** distance. It is between **four and five in the** afternoon when **he turns out of the High Street into** the quiet country road which is **to take him to** Cheswold. Light showers have refreshed **the verdure, the low** water meadows are looking **their greenest,** and the grassy hills yonder shut **out the world beyond this** fertile valley, and **give a look of security** and repose to the landscape, **so simply rustic,** so thoroughly English in its character. An hour later, and Alexis stands at the entrance to the village churchyard, a turnstile at a corner of the wall. He remembers this very path across the churchyard as a short cut to the Grange; and after nearly twenty years' absence the scene comes back to his memory as vividly as if he had left the place but yesterday. Yes, there stands the old yew tree, whose widely stretching boughs rustle and creak against the window by the pulpit in boisterous weather. No busy work of restoration is going on here. The greenish glass of the old diamond-paned casements has not been exchanged for the brilliant colouring of the modern glass-painter. The rough-cast walls are unchanged.

There is the wooden dial that used to mark the flight of time when he was a boy. There stands the old family tomb, neglected, forgotten, under its ivy shroud.

He lingers by the gate for some few minutes in a contemplative mood, looking dreamily at the well-remembered picture. Then he turns the stile and goes in.

He crosses the churchyard, looking idly at the

tombstones on either side the path, and within a few paces of the lych-gate he is brought to a standstill by a tablet that tells him **his visit to his cousin has** been deferred too **long**.

A massive granite slab, surmounted by **a** cross in white marble, bears this inscription :—

In Memory of

M A T I L D A ,

Only Daughter and Heiress of Mark Horatio Secretan,

Who died at Cheswold Grange, August 14th, 186—,

Aged Eighty-two Years

Matilda **Secretan** has been dead exactly **a year,** and the friendly grasp **of a** kindred hand **which** Alexis **has** hoped **for is** not for him.

'Poor **old** lady,' he sighs. 'Well, she **has** lived **her** life, and a good long one. An easy, **harm-** less, passionless existence, full of creature comforts **and** village dignity. **She was a** great person in Cheswold. Perhaps **it is** wiser to play at greatness in a rural village **than to struggle to** be really great amidst **the press** of men—pleasant to be born and **die on** one's **own** estate, to lie in one's shroud in the **same room in** which **one** was rocked in one's cradle

—to look out with our dying eyes upon the green fields in which we learned to walk, our own fields, not gained by toil or greed, or overreaching our fellow-men, but coming to us naturally as the blossoms come to the apple trees in our orchard. Yes, it must be a peaceful, pleasant life, affording no opportunity for sin. Satan must have a bad time among small landed proprietors. Poor cousin Matilda! I wonder who has come in for her property?'

The Grange lies within ten minutes' walk, just on the outer edge of the village. Alexis crosses the green, with its duck-pond, its groups of ancient elms before the good old village inn, with the 'Rising Sun,' looking very much like a careful representation of a mustard plaster, swinging from the signpost. A low white house this village inn, with a sloping thatch and a wonderful display of intensely red geraniums in intensely red flower-pots, a perfect blaze of scarlet floriculture.

Beyond the green and the 'Rising Sun' the road is shaded by fine old timber, and has a secluded look, as if one had strayed unawares into a gentleman's park. The hedgerows are so neatly cut, the grass margin of the road looks as if it had been mowed and rolled. There is a pleasant odour of pine woods. A little further on there comes an opening in the wooded screen, and across a running brook Alexis sees the wide park-like meadow which lies in front of Cheswold Grange. A sunk fence divides the grass land from the old-fashioned Grange garden ; and to the left of the long low old house, with its many gables, its dovecotes and bell-turret, lies the orchard, whose treasures are guarded by a thick holly hedge of two centuries' growth.

How well Alexis remembers the house ! a hospitable dwelling in the days of his boyhood, but somewhat gloomy of aspect now. Everything has a neglected air. He can see that even at a distance.

'I suppose Miss Secretan's heir despises the old place,' he thinks, 'and suffers the Grange to go to ruin, while he squanders the revenue of the land in London. I wonder who the fellow is? Some Low Church parson, perhaps, or smooth-tongued doctor, who got to the blind side of cousin Matilda at the last.'

He is at the lodge gate by this time. Even the lodge has a decayed air, a broken pane conspicuous in the parlour window, paint blistered, a bit of rotten gutter hanging from an angle of the roof.

'It looks like an Irish squireen's place in the bad old times fifty years ago,' thinks Alexis.

The lodgekeeper's wife is spreading out the weekly wash on the sunward side of a quickset hedge, and to this busy housewife Alexis addresses himself.

'You've a pretty place here,' he begins, with the casual air of an uninterested stranger. 'Pity it shouldn't be kept up a little better.'

'Ah, it is a pity,' answers the woman, shaking her head over the family linen. 'Things was very different in Miss Secretan's time.' She says this with the conviction that every one upon earth—the wandering stranger included—must know all about Miss Secretan. They may not have had the honour of that lady's acquaintance, but she must be known to them by reputation as one of the magnates of the land, just as Disraeli and Gladstone are known.

'She was a good mistress?' hazards Alexis.

'Ah,' sighs the woman, seeming to wring her hands as she **wrings out a** garment before unfurling it on the hedge, 'few like **her**. I won't **say but** what **she was near.** A lady that wouldn't allow the waste of a candle **end, and wore a** dress from year's end to year's end—but a silk as might **stand** alone. And them **as is** nearest towards theirselves is oftentimes kindest to others. Miss Secretan was a **kind** friend to many. She could do more kindness with sixpence than some people can do with half a crown. And she left a very **pretty property.** A pity it should go into Chancery.'

'Is it in Chancery?' **asks** Alexis, warmly interested.

'Well, I can't **say as it** is azackley, but it's something that way, I believe. You **see, Miss** Secretan, she makes her will a good twenty year ago, and she leaves **all** her property to a favourite nephew, or cousin, I'm not certain which, in trust for him if she should die before he came of age, but he was **to have** it handed over to him clear of everything if he **was** past twenty-one. And she never altered that will. She had thoughts of altering it,

I've heard Mrs. Bodlow, the housekeeper, say, because of her nephew not paying her the attention she expected ; but once having taken a good bit of trouble to make her will, she didn't care about beginning all over again. "I'll wait," says she—as I had it from Mrs. Bodlow,—"and I dare say," she says, "as one of these odd days," says she, "he'll remember me," she says, "and come and see me," says she ; "and if not," says she, "I'm hale and hearty still," she says, "and there's time enough to alter my will," says she, which Mrs. Bodlow repeated to me word batum while she was lying a corpse in that room with the three windows as you may see from here.'

Alexis has turned from red to pale and pale to red again during the progress of this prolix relation. The lodgekeeper's wife only pauses for breath ere she pursues her argument.

'So the will was let stand,' she resumes, 'and Miss Secretan didn't so much as trouble herself to find out whether the young man was living or dead ; and lo and behold ! when the will was made known, the heir was nowheres to be found. I believe the

lawyers and such like did all as was proper, and he
was advertised to his advantage in the newspapers
continual, but he never answered none of the adver-
tisements, which he couldn't have failed to do if he
was alive and could write—unless he'd gone out to
Horsetralyer and turned butcher like that simple-
'arted young gentleman as you read of in the newspapers. Howsomedever, there's the property, belonging to no one, as you may say, and things going to
ruin. There's one gardener kept to grub about a bit,
where there used to be two men and a by at work
constant, and there's a pore 'elpless old woman in
the 'ouse, with 'ardly strength to open a shutter and
let in a breath of hair, so you may guess as the
moths are having their free will of the damass
curtings and such like.'

'You didn't hear the name of the heir,' says
Alexis, interrogatively.

'Not his chrisen name. His other name was the
same as hern. "I'll have a Secretan to come after me
if I can," she says, and Mrs. Bodlow told me as she
believed it was mostly on account of the name as
Miss Secretan left that young man the property.'

Alexis tries his hardest to still the troubled beating of his heart, tries to persuade himself that it is too soon to feel the flush and pride of sudden unexpected fortune.   Matilda Secretan may have had other cousins, or nephews, he tells himself.   He is not particularly well posted in the family history, having heard his father prose about his kindred with youth's heedless ear.   He tells himself it is too soon to be glad, yet he feels as if he were lord of the soil. He stands within the gate, and he plants his foot firmly on the ground.

'I wonder if I am standing on my own land?' he thinks.   'I feel as if there were a glow in the soil that communicates itself to my blood.   It is the land that has belonged to my race for three hundred years.'

The fact that for the space of a year no one has come forward to claim the property encourages the supposition that he himself is the missing heir.

'Would it be possible for me to see the house? he inquires, seized with a feverish desire to examine the mansion which may or may not be his.

'I dare say if you was to offer the old lady a

trifle, she wouldn't mind letting you see it, sir. She's a little hard of hearing.'

'Suppose I offer you five shillings to begin with,' suggests Alexis, dropping two half-crowns into the matron's hand. 'You might take me up to the house and make things square with the old lady.'

The lodgekeeper's face beams all over with delight. 'I'm sure I'm much beholden to you, sir. I'll dry my hands directly minute, and step up to the great house with you.'

The Grange has been 'the great house' at Cheswold for generations.

'Oh, Sibyl,' thinks Alexis as he walks along the grassy path under the elms, 'if you had only waited for brighter days, how happy we might have been! You abandon me in order to seek fortune, and you don't seem to have won it yet. Fortune falls into my lap unsought.'

The fact of his wife's desertion seems harder to him in the face of this sudden turn of fortune's wheel than it has seemed before. That prosperity should come to him thus, and find him a lonely man!

If this estate of Cheswold has been actually left him, shall he lure his wife back to him by a golden bait? Shall he win from his altered fortunes the boon that has been refused to a husband's entreaty? No, a thousand times no. 'If she comes back to me ever she shall return to the pauper she abandoned,' he tells himself. 'She shall come back for love of me her husband, not to be mistress of Cheswold Grange.'

Yet how proud he would be, having won her back to her duty, to point to this peaceful old English home, and say, 'I am no longer an adventurer and a beggar. All this is ours, and our children's after us!' He has quite made up his mind by this time that he is the missing heir, and that these elms which screen him from the low western sun are his very own.

Cheswold Grange upon this August evening has a mouldy smell, and wears the gloomy and somewhat ghostly aspect of a house whose shutters are for the most part closed against air and sunshine. But it is a good old house notwithstanding. The rooms are large, the staircase is wide and substantial, with fine carved oak balusters, an open gallery above with numerous doors, suggestive of ample accommodation for a family. The quaint old furniture remains just as Miss Secretan left it. Chairs and sofas are carefully shrouded in holland, and the dust lies thick upon the old rosewood tables, the Canton porcelain, and the crystal chandeliers, whose half-burned wax candles shed their light upon the vanished mistress of the Grange.

'Nothing has been touched,' says Mrs. Cramp, of the lodge, as she follows Alexis and the old woman in charge from room to room. 'Everythink is the same as in Miss Secretan's time, except that when she was living you couldn't have found a grain of dust in the place if you'd offered a five-pound note for it.'

After having looked at the house Alexis explores stables and gardens. It is dark by the time his inspection is finished, and he makes up his mind to spend the night at the 'Rising Sun' in Cheswold village. He feels attached to the place already.

'Is there much land belonging to the Grange?' he inquires of Mrs. Cramp, the old woman in charge

being little more than a dummy, and Mrs. Cramp
serving as interpreter.

'I can't say how many acres, sir, though I dare
say my husband might know if he was at home.
There's Baker's farm, and there's the Hollow farm
and the Hill farm—that must be a good bit
altogether.   Miss Secretan was lady of the manor.'

This is pleasant to hear.   Alexis gratifies the
deaf caretaker with his bounty, and goes back to the
gate with Mrs. Cramp, who enlarges upon the
beauties of the place, and asks him if he has any
idea of taking the property if it should be to let.

'Chancery might just as well let the great house,
you see, sir, if it was only for the sake of having it
took care of.   It would be all the better for the heir
if he should come to claim his own.   It went to my
heart to see things so dusty.   And I hope, sir, if
you should have any thoughts of the place you'll
keep on me and my good man at the lodge.   We
served Miss Secretan faithful above eleven years.'

'I won't displace you, Mrs. Cramp, you may rely
on it, if I should ever come to be master of Cheswold Grange.   Good night.   Oh, by the way,' he adds,

just as he is turning to go, 'do you happen to know the name of Miss Secretan's lawyer?'

'Mr. Scrodgers, of Winchester, sir. Scrodgers and Son it is now.'

'Thanks. Good night again.'

'He must be thinking of taking the place,' muses Mrs. Cramp, 'or he wouldn't want to see Mr. Scrodgers.'

Alexis finds the 'Rising Sun' a comfortable old hostelry of a primitive style. Dinner resolves itself into tea and eggs and bacon, but the eggs and bacon are admirable, the home-made loaf delicious, and the cream-jug which accompanies the teapot suggests a land flowing with milk and honey. The parlour in which the traveller enjoys this homely meal is clean and bright, and adjoins the bar so closely that Alexis can carry on a conversation with the landlord as he takes his refreshment. From this gentleman he hears that Cheswold Grange is one of the nicest little estates in the county, worth fifteen hundred a year at the lowest computation, and that Miss Secretan was a careful old lady, and must have saved money.

'How could she spend much, you see, sir? living in her quiet way, never leaving home from year's end to year's end, growing her own meat, and making her own butter, and having everything in a ring fence, as you may say. Ah, there'll be a pretty tidy bit of rhino for that young man to come into if they ever find him.'

That young man—or the young man who supposes himself to be the heir—feels a thrill of satisfaction at the idea, and is somewhat impatient for to-morrow morning and an interview with Messrs. Scrodgers and Son.

'Do you know much about Mr. Scrodgers of Winchester, the old lady's solicitor?' asks Alexis.

'Not much, sir, I'm happy to say. I keeps aloof from that cattle. Not as I've ever heard any harm of Scrodgers and Son, but they're all tarred with the same brush, to my mind. If you've got a bit of freehold property, they wants you to mortgage it just to give them something to do. If you've got a bit of property to leave, they wants you to throw it into hodge-podge, just to give them the 'andling of it, and if they can get you into Chancery body and bones, they do it, for the good of trade. No lawyers for me, sir, but I believe as lawyers go, Scrodgers and Son are very decent fellows.'

Alexis sleeps peacefully that night, better than he has slept since he landed in the port of London, and is closeted with Mr. Scrodgers the elder early next morning, in the quiet front parlour of a substantial old house in a side street in Winchester The office has a respectable and well-to-do look, and Mr. Scrodgers is white-bearded and venerable enough for an abbot. The grave cathedral over-shadows his dwelling, and increases the respect-ability of his surroundings.

Alexis has sent in his card :—

> ALEXIS SECRETAN,
>> Agent for Messrs. Keel & Skrew,
>>> SIDNEY.

The lawyer receives him politely, with a manner that is half friendly, half suspicious.

'May I ask what Mr. Secretan I have the pleasure of addressing ?' he inquires, looking at the card.

'I don't quite know how you would wish me to describe myself. I am the son of Philip Secretan, who died at Nice in 1858, and who was first cousin of Miss Secretan of Cheswold Grange. I come to you, Mr. Scrodgers, to inquire about my cousin's will. I have been in Australia for the last two years, acting as agent for a house in the City, and I only became aware of my cousin Matilda's death yesterday evening.'

'This is very serious,' says Mr. Scrodgers, looking at Alexis as if he should like to convict him as an impostor. 'And pray how did you come to hear of Miss Secretan's demise yesterday evening, not having heard of it prior to that time? May I ask how the intelligence reached you finally?'

Mr. Scrodgers rubs his hands complacently after this address, and fixes Alexis with his large gray eyes, which are of the protuberant order.

'The knowledge came to me in the simplest possible manner. I went over to Cheswold intending to pay my cousin a visit, and found her name on a tombstone in the churchyard.'

'Are you quite sure, sir, that the fact of Miss

Secretan's death did not become known to you in Australia, and did not influence your return to this country?' inquires the lawyer, severely.

'If you think me an impostor, Mr. Scrodgers, I will thank you to say so plainly, and I will take means to establish my identity. This beating about the bush is as insulting to my understanding as it is to my honour.'

'This is a very serious business, Mr. Secretan, a good deal more serious than you may suppose. We are entrusted with a great responsibility, sir. If we err it must be on the side of caution.'

'You mean that my cousin Matilda left the whole of her property to Alexis Secretan, and you doubt whether I am the man, although I put his name upon my card.'

'It would be for you to establish your identity, Mr. Secretan.'

'Nothing more easy. My father's solicitors, Messrs. Gull and Sharpe, of Lincoln's Inn Fields, have been familiar with every stage of my existence up to the time when I sold my commission, about five years ago. They hold all family documents—

certificates of baptism, and so on. My father was a careless man as to business matters, but he had infinite faith in his lawyers, and he committed all papers of any significance into their charge.'

'Messrs. Gull and Sharpe are a most respectable firm,' answers Mr. Scrodgers, with a reverential expression of countenance, as if so old-established a firm ought to be spoken of with awe.

'I refer you to them for my identification,' says Alexis, 'and I shall be obliged if you will let them have a copy of my cousin's will. I shall go to them directly I get back to London, and take all necessary steps under their advice.'

'I have not offended you, I hope, Mr. Secretan, by my business-like manner of discussing this question. I had the honour to enjoy Miss Secretan's confidence for many years, and I am naturally ——'

'Very naturally—quite proper. Good morning, Mr. Scrodgers. Please lose no time about the copy of my cousin's will.

'The original document is in Doctors' Commons.'

'Ah, then, Gull and Sharpe will be able to get me a copy. Good morning.'

Alexis leaves the dull old office elate. He knows all that he wanted to know—knows that he is lord of Cheswold Grange ; that he need never go back to Australia; that his agency for Keel and Skrew is at an end; that he is an Englishman of landed estate—a gentleman by fortune as he is a gentleman by birth.

He is eager to get back to London, if it were only to communicate his good fortune to the friend of his adversity, Richard Plowden.

'Dear old Dick ! how glad he will be ! He shall have an acre of ferns at Cheswold, and his mother need never let lodgings any more unless she likes.'

There is one thought that touches him most deeply, —the thought of the child whose face he has never seen.

CHAPTER VI.

STARTLING INFORMATION.

AIDED by Messrs. Gull and Sharpe, of the Fields,
who put all things in train for him, and take him
under their parchment wing with affectionate protection, Alexis has no difficulty in proving his right
to Cheswold Grange, and all those messuages and
tenements and various holdings thereto appertaining.
It is a comfortable estate to inherit, for Miss Secretan has been an admirable woman of business,
and has managed everything with fostering care
which has beautified and enriched all it touched.
The land—save five-and-thirty acres of home farm,
park-like pasturage all of it—is let on long leases
to tenants who are contented with their holdings, and
do not grudge labour or money on improvements.
The gardens, the house, the stables, need only a little
care to restore them to that perfection of elegant
precision and graceful order which distinguished
them during Miss Secretan's lifetime. Alexis takes

a singular mode of restoring things, and one which
wins him much favour from the inhabitants of
Cheswold and its immediate neighbourhood. He
contrives, with considerable trouble to himself, to
get back all his cousin's old servants,—the butler
or indoor servant, pompous as the ruler over a
retinue of powdered footmen, yet with only one
small underling in the shape of a knife-boy; Mrs.
Bodlow, the cook and housekeeper, who had served
Miss Secretan five-and-twenty years; the middle-
aged housemaid, who had polished every article of
furniture in the low-ceiled bedchambers so often
that each had become an object of affection and
pride to her; the gardeners, who knew every apple
tree, every plum and peach, nectarine and apricot on
the old red walls; the coachman, who had driven
Miss Secretan about in the old-fashioned barouche,
a serviceable vehicle yet, and in the old green pony
chaise, and had ultimately subsided into drawing
her along the shady lanes in a Bath chair. Alexis
feels a pride in restoring the scattered household—
in seeing every bit of furniture, every quaint old
ornament assume its proper place. How intensely

had Matilda Secretan studied the fitness of things before she so placed them—the Chelsea shepherdess at this angle, the Wedgwood teapot on that shelf, that figure of Quin as Falstaff in Bow china to balance Kitty Clive in Worcestershire ware, and so on to the end of the modest collection. Alexis remembers how his childish eyes had gloated on the old china—how those household treasures had seemed to him more beautiful than anything he had ever seen before. He remembers the garden—the broad gravel walk leading to a Dutch summerhouse, in red brick, with stained glass windows—the orange trees in square green tubs ranged along the closely shorn grass that had once served as a bowling-green. The place is very dear to him, for it recalls the happiest days of his childhood.

Before the elms in the avenue have quite lost their summer green in the early days of a fine September, Alexis is established at the Grange; the old servants have come back, and everything is in order. Full of delight in his new possessions the master of Cheswold Grange invites Richard Plowden to come and shoot his partridges.

'They are my partridges,' he adds, 'though they feed on my tenants' corn for the most part. Come and have a pop at them, Dick,'—an invitation which startles Mr. Plowden, who has never fired a gun in his life.

Dick comes to Cheswold Grange, however, and gladly, not to pop at the partridges, but to rejoice in the sight of his old friend and patron, basking in prosperity's sunshine.

'I always felt you must be born to good luck, Captain Secretan——'

'Call me Alex, Dick, or I shall hit you.'

'Well, then, Alex. There was something so bright and genial about you. It seemed as if you couldn't long be under a cloud.'

'Did it, Dick? The cloudy weather lasted quite long enough though, old fellow, and the clouds are not gone yet. It's a hard thing to have this beautiful place, and not be able to bring my baby boy here, and establish him in the home which is to be his when I am dead and gone.'

'Have you told your wife of your altered fortunes?' inquires Dick.

'Not a word. She shall know me only as the pauper she deserted, or I will at best own to the wages of a hard-working clerk. She shall come back to my poverty, Dick, if she and I are ever to be reunited—not to my wealth. How pretty she would look at the head of this table, by the way!'

They are lounging over their wine after dinner, the diamond-cut decanters reflected in the polished mahogany as in dark water, golden egg-plums from the western wall, and peaches from the southern, nestling among dark green leaves in heart-shaped dishes of old Derby china.

'Yes, I dare say,' says Dick, more inclined to blame than to praise the absent wife.

'You never saw her, Dick. A pity. She is so lovely—a woman created for happiness and prosperity, not for toil and care. And in marrying me she wedded poverty and sorrow. It was very hard for her. I ought to have been more considerate. Can I wonder that she grew weary of the struggle—that she tried to cut the knot that bound her to my misfortunes? Poor child!'

'Poor you, I think, to have wedded such a piece of selfish prettiness,' says Dick.

'Don't be hard upon her, Dick. Fortune was too unkind in those days. The outlook was so black. If there had been a glimmer of hope on our horizon she would have stayed with me, I've no doubt. Think of her now, drudging as a governess, hiding her beauty in some back parlour, or second-floor nursery—toiling for a pittance, while I enjoy all the comforts of this dear old place. That's hard to think of, isn't it, old fellow?'

'Merely retributive justice,' answers Dick, sturdily. 'But are you sure that she is a governess now?'

'I have every reason to suppose so. Her last letter tells me that she is on the high road to fortune —fortune which she and I are to share. Taking this in conjunction with the information I got from her sister, I can only imagine that she is in the employment of some rich person likely to leave her money.'

'Rather an ignoble position that,' says Dick,— 'waiting for dead men's shoes.'

Alexis sighs, and pours out another glass of his cousin's well-kept La Rose.

'What are you going to do to find her?' asks Richard.

'I've put the business in the hands of a very clever man in London, to whom my lawyers recommended me. In the abstract I hate the idea of a private inquiry office, but in my particular case I can't get on without one. My man is to find out Sibyl's whereabouts by hook or by crook. Once found, and face to face with her, I don't think I should be long in bringing her to reason. She must have changed very much if she has ceased to love me.'

Dick ventures no reply to this. He has a very poor opinion of his friend's wife, thinks her stony-hearted, nay, almost inhuman, and in his idea Alexis Secretan's future happiness would be best secured by Sibyl's being kept at a distance. What could be sweeter than life in this old country house, among these fertile gardens, these park-like meadows? and why disturb the serenity of the atmosphere by bringing a woman here? The lovelier she is, the more trouble she is likely to bring. Was it not Helen's beauty which overturned a world ?

Mr. Secretan's new life is assuredly so full of pleasantness, that if it were possible for him to forget the wife he has loved, or to cease from longing for the son he has never seen, he might reasonably take his ease and enjoy the pleasures of a tranquil mind. Cheswold seems to him just one of the most delightful places on the surface of this earth. It is set in a landscape of rural beauty, fertile, luxuriant, like a picture of Constable's. There is plenty of sport, a good pack of foxhounds in the neighbourhood, to which Alexis subscribes liberally. There are pleasant neighbours, who hasten to call upon the inheritor of Cheswold Grange, and are eager to make themselves useful.

Mr. Secretan finds himself received with such peculiar cordiality by fathers and mothers of goodly families of grown-up daughters that he takes an early opportunity to let it be known that he is that worst of detrimentals, a husband without a wife. He tells one of his new friends, in the strictest confidence, that he is temporarily separated from his wife in consequence of some family quarrel, but he hopes for reunion before very long ; and in a week everybody within twenty miles of Cheswold knows all about it. The disappointment is rather severe for the parents of marriageable daughters, some of whom have been hanging rather long on hand, like the winter pears on the wall. Mr. Secretan is not a great catch in the matrimonial market, of course. A pretty old house and grounds and from fifteen hundred to two thousand a year. A very moderate alliance, but a comfortable and a respectable one, think the anxious parents. And then Miss Secretan has always ranked high among her neighbours. There is an odour of sanctity about the Grange.

'A pity the young fellow should have made such a mess of himself,' remark the fathers. The mothers go so far as to call it a shame. The daughters feel a sense of loss, and are not quite so amiable to Mr. Secretan the next time he takes them in to dinner.

Old friends whom he knew in his days of youthful extravagance find him out, and rejoice in his restored fortunes. A couple of old brother

officers crop up in the neighbourhood. Colonel
Churton settled and sobered into a country gentleman, great in the cultivation of mangold and
turnips; Major Tollinson, who breeds prize cattle,
which help to eat the colonel's roots;—these are
full of warmest friendliness.

It seems to Alexis as if he had never been
poor. He has spent some of his cousin's accumu-
lated cash in the payment of his debts—debts
of honour and tradesmen's bills have alike been
repaid, with five per cent. interest in every case.
There is now no one living who can say he has
lost money by Alexis Secretan.

'What a pleasant feeling it is, Dick!' says
Alexis, as he pockets the last receipt, "with respectful thanks." 'I really feel as if I had only just
reached my proper number of inches, as if I had
been half a head shorter than I ought to be for the
last six years. There is a springiness in my step,
too. Ah, Dick, this is the real worth of money—
"the glorious privilege of being independent.'"

Alexis has settled down comfortably in the
rooms he has chosen for himself, and begins to

feel as if he had lived at the Grange all his life
by the time the first frosts sparkle on the grass,
and the leaves fall fast from the good old trees,
and lie thick in grove and glade, despite of gardeners and wheelbarrows. He has put up new
bookshelves in the library, where Miss Secretan's
favourite poets and divines, in neat calf or vellum
bindings, make but a small appearance, and has
filled them with the books he loves, a truly
cosmopolitan collection. He has bought himself a
couple of clever hunters, and a useful covert hack,
which he can also drive in a dogcart. He has
shot over the stubbles, and in the preserves of his
noble neighbour, Lord Starborough, and has had
two or three good runs with the foxhounds. He
has made a large circle of new acquaintances,
and renewed several old friendships. But in
all this time he has had no tidings of Sibyl.

He has, it is true, received numerous letters
from the private inquiry office, some promising
speedy success, others asking some questions of
detail, which might help to confirm a suspicion, or
establish its falsehood, some declaring that the in-

quirer is on the right track. But the result has been failure. So far private inquiry has effected **nothing.**

Despairing of ever succeeding by this means, Alexis inserts an advertisement, which he means to be his final appeal to his obdurate wife.

'Dixon Street, Chelsea.—I refuse to write to you through the faithful servant in L—— Street. I consider such indirect communication degrading to you and to me. I have no sympathy with your schemes. I decline any share in fortune so won. I claim you by my sacred right as your husband. You need not fear starvation, or even the pinch of poverty. I have obtained employment which will enable me to keep my wife and child in decent comfort. Come back, and be assured of my fondest affection. Prolong our separation, and it may become eternal.'

This advertisement is quickly answered by another, beginning with the watchword, Dixon Street.

'Wait and hope. A little patience, and we shall be reunited. You cannot wish for reunion more earnestly than I do. The fabric which has taken more than two years to build must not be destroyed by a moment of impatience.'

Alexis inserts a second advertisement.

'Dixon Street.—Give me the custody of our son, and I will be content.'

To which the answer is one word—

'Impossible.'

On this Mr. Secretan loses temper, and love gives way to resentment.

'Heartless, inexorable!' he says to himself. 'She loves money better than she loves me. The sordid desire to inherit some weak-minded old woman's wealth is stronger with her than duty or affection. Is she worth all the pain I have suffered for her? Is she worthy the constancy I have given her?'

The answer to these questions is a decided negative. His love for his wife has been a foolish, unreasoning passion, wasted upon an unworthy object. He now determines to forget that cold and cruel wife, and to enjoy all the pleasures of his new position; and in the various employments and engagements of country life his

days glide by smoothly and pleasantly until the
approach of Christmas. It is now three years
since Sibyl left him. He dines with Colonel
Churton one bright frosty evening, just a week
before the Christian festival. The colonel's spacious
old house, Longley Mead, is full of guests, military
and civil, young people, middle-aged people,
elderly people, pretty girls, with portly mothers
and portlier fathers.

They sit down, about thirty, to dinner, in a fine
oak-paneled dining-room, and the board is a merry
and noisy one. Quiet flirtation is going on doubtless in some quarters under cover of the general
talk and laughter, the cross-firing of respectable old
jokes, the remarkable anecdotes of horses, dogs,
foxes, and birds; the discussion of that last troublesome case at petty sessions, and a good deal more
genuine county talk. The banquet is long and
splendid; but at last the ice puddings have made
their round, the liqueurs have followed in fairy
goblets, golden-starred, the hothouse grapes have
been admired, and the ladies have left the ruder sex
to draw up to the host's end of the long table, and

enter upon that serious discussion of the merits of various Burgundies and Bordeaux, which appears to afford so much delight to the masculine mind.

'You used to be a pretty good judge of claret in your time, Secretan,' says the colonel, cheerily, 'give me your candid opinion of that Margaux.'

'About as good a judge of claret as he was of a pretty woman,' says Major Tollinson, while Alexis gravely sips the Château Margaux, 'and he had a wonderful eye for beauty.'

'Oh, come, now,' remonstrates the colonel, 'Secretan was never a ladies' man. He left that kind of thing to you, Tollinson.'

'Oh, I grant that he was too lazy a beggar to play croquet on a blazing July afternoon, or to dance attendance at picnics or tea-fights, or make himself useful at a school feast, carrying baskets of buns and jugs of boiling tea. But he was a great admirer of the sex for all that, and at a county ball he always got the most dances with the prettiest women.'

'A nice clean wine,' says Alexis, ignoring these remarks.

'Talking of pretty women,' says a young man who

sits furthest from the host, 'I think I had the pleasure of meeting one of the prettiest girls you could ever hope to see, down in Yorkshire the week before last.'

The word Yorkshire catches the ear of Alexis. So large a county must needs be rich in female beauty; but he remembers that Redcastle is in Yorkshire, and thinks of Sibyl. Or perhaps it is that instinct which in some moments of our lives warns us that some word vital to our interests is about to be spoken.

'Plenty of pretty women in Yorkshire,' says the host, incuriously. 'How did you find the grouse this year, Danvers? You were staying somewhere near the moors, I suppose.'

'No, I was in rather a poor country for grouse. I was at Mr. Holford's place between Hillsborough and Redcastle.'

Alexis grows pale, and refills his glass with a hand that shakes a little.

'May we ask for the beauty's name?' he says.

'She is a Miss Faunthorpe—an heiress, I believe. At least, there's a rich old East Indian party she goes about with, and I conclude she's to have his money, by-and-bye. I met her at a dinner at Sir Wilford Cardonnel's, and the rumour is that Sir Wilford is going to marry her. He's uncommonly sweet upon her, that's a fact patent to the meanest comprehension.'

Alexis tries to check the tumultuous beating of his heart, tries to steady himself and compose his countenance, and by a great effort succeeds.

Why should this be his false wife? asks the voice of reason. Sibyl has a grown-up sister whom he has never seen, a sister who may be as lovely as herself, although his wife always disparaged Marion's charms. Or this Miss Faunthorpe may belong to some other family—nay, must so belong, since she is spoken of as an heiress.

"You have roused my warmest interest in this Yorkshire beauty,' he says, with assumed languor. 'Could you not draw upon your powers so far as to describe her to us?'

'Yes, by all means. Indulge us with a little word-painting; give us a verbal photograph of your beauty,' says Colonel Churton.

' Who can describe the indescribable ? ' exclaims Mr. Danvers, pleased at having made himself the object of general attention, after having languished in the shade during the rest of the entertainment.

' Picture to yourselves——'

' Oh, come, we want you to do the picturing——'

' Imagine an oval face framed in dark brown hair, loosely braided—I believe that's the word, isn't it ? Hair with a glimmer of gold and a natural ripple, eyes of darkest brown, complexion ivory pale, save when excitement flushes the cheek with a lovely pink, like the inside of those pomegranates ; features almost Grecian.'

' Sounds rather like a face in a fashion plate,' says Major Tollinson. ' I'd rather hear of a *retrousse* nose, red hair and freckles, or a tawny little gipsy with murderous black eyes.'

' Not to admire Miss Faunthorpe would be to despise perfection,' says Mr. Danvers, slightly offended.

' You haven't told us her Christian name,' says Alexis.

' ' It fits her to a nicety, for there is a mystic look

about her pale face and dark brown eyes.   Her
name is Sibyl.'

'And she is going to be married to a Yorkshire
baronet ? '

'Sir Wilford Cardonnel, one of the wealthiest
land owners in the West Riding.   Mind, I don't say
the match is a settled thing.   It hasn't been for-
mally announced, you know; people haven't begun
to congratulate her; but the marriage is talked of.
I dare say the local papers will get hold of it soon.
" We understand," &c.'

'And there is a rich uncle in question ? ' asks
Alexis.   He has recovered his self-command by
this time, and makes the inquiry with the air of
a man who only talks for the sake of keeping up
the conversation.

'Yes, a shrivelled old fellow, who eats any
amount of Nepaul pepper.   An artful old bird !
Looks as if he had made his money in slaves, or
opium, or something contraband.   Sort of man
who would have done well in Warren Hastings'
time, when John Company had things all his own
way in the East.'

'Do you remember his name?'

'Let me see—hum—ha—er—er—Travers—no —rather an odd name. Trinder. No. Trenchard. Yes, that's it. Stephen Trenchard. Pretty niece called him sometimes uncle Stephen, sometimes uncle Trenchard.'

'Stephen Trenchard,' repeats Alexis, staring blankly at the tall epergne in front of him.

This is a shock he was not prepared for. Stephen Trenchard, his father's bitter enemy. The man whose arts disinherited him, Alexis, while yet unborn. The man whom his family religion taught him to execrate. And it was this man's niece—a daughter of this detested race—he had married It was to court and cherish his father's enemy that his wife had left him.

'This is the fortune she is to inherit and we are to share. This is the scheme of her life. It is for Stephen Trenchard's ill-gotten wealth I am to wait. It is for this I am to be patient and trust her. And she shows herself so true to her trust that common rumour gives her to another man. It is time for me to make an end of this farce of fidelity.'

BEFORE the close of the next day Alexis is once more in Redcastle. This time, however, he goes straight to the chief inn, or hotel, as it proudly calls itself,—the institution which supports and sustains the languishing spirits of the half-dozen or so of idle young men who adorn Redcastle by their residence. The hotel affords them a porch, or portico, in which to lounge and gossip with one another, or for want of more aristocratic company, with the landlord of the establishment, who appears to have nothing to do, from morn till dewy eve, but stand on his threshold and survey the varieties of life as presented by Below Bar and the market-place, where a pedestrian may be seen to pass once in five minutes, and a vehicle of some description may be reckoned upon once in half an hour. Besides this portico, or school of conversation, which is in a manner a free institution, the 'Coach and Horses' furnishes its patrons with a bar in which to imbibe mild admixtures of soda water and brandy, appetising sherry and bitters, or the more economic re-freshment of a glass of ale, while two lively bar-maids, gifted with a considerable power of repartee, stimulate the native youth to intellectual effort. On one side of the hotel is the billiard-room, where awful contests of skill go on under the shaded lamps, and money is won and lost. On the other side is the reading room, where, besides a variety of useful information in the way of Bradshaw's guides, the county history, almanacks, and time tables, the lounger may enjoy literature as fresh as the day before yesterday's *Evening Standard*, or a *Punch* not quite three weeks old.

At the 'Coach and Horses,' Alexis deposits his small valise this dark December evening at five o'clock, the universal tea time among the burgesses and lower classes of Redcastle, the witching hour at which Mrs. Stormont and her friends discuss the morals and finances of their neighbours over harle-quin cups of orange pekoe. He has come to the hotel in order to draw breath before swooping down upon that false wife of his, and with a view, perhaps to making himself better acquainted with the ground he stands upon. From Mr. Danvers he may have heard something less or something more than the truth. Here, in the place she inhabits, he is likely to make himself acquainted with the best or the worst that men and women can say of her.

He bitterly resents the falsehoods told him by Jenny Faunthorpe nearly six months ago. That instance of juvenile depravity is only a new proof of the bad blood that flows in the veins of the Trenchards. Alexis looks upon it as hereditary vice.

' They are all cold-hearted and false alike,' he tells himself. ' The man robbed my father of his rights, and wore a smooth face all the time, and pretended to be his friend. The child looks in my face and lies to me. Who could have suspected a child of such falsehood ? '

Being set upon by an elderly waiter, and besought to order his dinner, Mr. Secretan expresses a provoking indifference to that meal. He will have anything they like to give him in an hour's time. A private sitting-room ? Yes, by all means, and a good fire. He will go for a walk while his dinner is preparing. And, by the way, which is Mr. Trenchard's house ?

' Mr. Trenchard's house ? Lancaster Lodge.' The waiter mentions it with respect in his tone. ' Straight up the street, sir, and through the Bar. It is the third house on your left above Bar. You can't miss it, sir. A noble-looking mansion, with a lodge entrance. One of the finest houses in Redcastle.'

Alexis strolls up the street in the winter dusk. Lamps gleam redly behind fanlights. There is a rosy fire-glow on some of the windows. The respectability of the scene strikes the stranger. It is so different from that dilapidated, untidy end of the town in which Dr. Faunthorpe's house is situated.

' So my wife has a rich uncle as well as a poor one; and she came back to her native town to pay her court to the rich man, not to seek a homely shelter with the poor one. And she knew that she was my enemy's niece, and had not candour or courage enough to tell me the truth. It suited her humour better to leave me in a sneaking fashion, and fasten herself on to the wealth of a scoundrel.'

So muses the outraged husband as he walks up the street, and under the old Gothic archway. Yes, there is Lancaster Lodge—ponderous, gloomy, looking like a moneyed man's house. There is no gleam of light in the upper windows, and the wall hides the lower. A jail or a reformatory would look more cheerful.

'Is she happy within those walls?' he asks, 'or is she like an enchanted princess shut up in a golden prison? She has bartered all things for the hope of wealth—honour, truth, affection—just as her uncle did before her.'

He has no mind to lose much time before standing face to face with his wife; but he wishes first to hear what the townspeople have to tell about her. How much truth is there in that rumour of an intended marriage? How much encouragement has she given to her admirer? At the 'Coach and Horses' they are likely to be well informed of all the local gossip, and at the 'Coach and Horses' he intends to make his inquiries.

He is shown into a sitting-room, spacious enough
for a party of twelve, and brilliantly illuminated.
The number of glasses, various in colour and shape,
which adorn the dinner-table, might be taken to
imply that he is expected to drink deeply of the
'Coach and Horses' wine.

On receiving his modest order of a pint of claret,
the waiter sweeps off champagne and hock glasses
in a low-spirited way, and relieves his disappointment with a faint cough.

The dinner is served in very good style, the
elderly waiter receiving the dishes at the door from
his subordinate, and sliding about the room stealth-
ily, as if he were attending to the wants of a dying
traveller, whose ebbing breath he was appointed to
watch.

Alexis dawdles over his fish, and dallies with his
cutlet and tomato sauce.

'Do you see much of Mr. Trenchard?' he
asks.

'Mr. Trenchard, sir? No, sir. Mr. Trenchard is
a very reserved kind of gentleman. He is much
sought after in Redcastle, and I believe he do attend

a good many dinner parties among first-class people ;
but as to playing billiards in our room downstairs, or
taking his glass of wine, or brandy and soda, he is
quite the last kind of gentleman. Besides which,
one may say that his age precludes that sort of thing,
although we have older gentlemen than Mr. Trenchard in our billiard-room. But he has a very fine
table of his own, you see, sir ; indeed, I may say he
drawed off one of our best customers with his table—
young Mr. Stormont, which used to come here almost
every evening, a poor player, but a genteel young
man. Very much taken with Mr. Trenchard's niece
he is, but there's not much hope for him in that
quarter,' adds the waiter, as he lowers the cover
on the cutlet dish, with a twirl of his arm like a
movement in the broadsword exercise.

'Why not ?' asks Alexis.

'Because the young lady looks higher, sir ; as
well she may, seeing that Mr. Frederick Stormont
hasn't one sixpence to rub against another, as the
saying is. Miss Faunthorpe is a beauty, sir—a
regular beauty ; and she's been told of it often
enough, I'll lay, to know how to set a right value

on herself. And then the old gentleman's sure to leave her his money. He's adopted her, you see, sir. There's other nieces down town, but this one's his fancy, and he's adopted her. Everybody knows she's to come into all his money. And now they say Sir Wilford Cardonnel's going to marry her, and she'll hold her head as high as any in the West Riding, for there isn't a finer gentleman than Sir Wilford between here and York.'

'Who says that she is to be married to Sir Wilford?'

'Everybody, sir, it's town talk. There's been plenty said about it downstairs in the billiard-room. They've chaffed young Mr. Stormont about it, and he do look uncommon miserable, poor young gentleman, when they go on at him, and tell him he's missed his chance with Miss Faunthorpe. "And if you don't marry an heiress, whatever are you to do to get your living, Fred?" says they. "Blest if I know," says he. "I'll tell you what, Fred," says Mr. Staples, the Vet, "you'll have to eat that horse of yours, or he'll have to eat you. It 'll come to that sooner or later, for you'll never be able to keep him." "I'm afraid it will," answers Mr Stormont, as meek as a lamb.'

Alexis is not warmly interested in the impression which Sibyl's intended marriage—or the rumour of such an intention—may have made upon Frederick Stormont. He is more concerned in its effect upon himself.

'And pray what kind of man is this Stephen Trenchard?' he asks presently. 'Is he liked in your town?'

'I don't know about liking,' replies the waiter, dubiously; 'the townspeople would hardly go to take such a liberty. He's very much looked up to.'

'Does he or the young lady—this pretty niece of his—do much good in the place?'

'Mr. Trenchard subscribes to our local charities, sir. Good, in the sense of districk visiting, or Sunday school teaching, or anything in that line, the young lady does not do. Her position raises her above that, you see, sir.'

'I understand. Active benevolence of that kind occupies a lower level.'

'Decidedly, sir. Young persons who have less

call upon their time can naturally devote themselves to school teaching and such like. Miss
Faunthorpe moves in the highest society—she visits
a great deal. It would be quite out of the
question ——'

'That she should trouble herself about the
welfare of her inferior fellow-creatures. Of course.
Well, I'll go and call at Lancaster Lodge. It's
rather late ; but as a traveller I may be excused
that informality.'

'You know Mr. Trenchard, sir ?' exclaims the
waiter, alarmed lest he should not have expressed
himself carefully enough about that great man,
although he has echoed those accents of adulation
which prevail in Redcastle whenever Stephen
Trenchard is mentioned.

'My father knew him—intimately,' replies Alexis.

It is between seven and eight when he rings the
bell at the lodge gate of Mr. Trenchard's mansion, a
fine winter's night. The stars are shining on lawn
and plane trees, shrubbery and empty flower-beds,
as the lodgekeeper shows Mr. Secretan the way to
the solemn pillared doorway.

Here a footman in livery, warned by the lodge-keeper's bell, receives the stranger. Very silent is the lamplit hall, where a bust of Wellington, on a porphyry pedestal, keeps company with a bust of Pitt the younger, on a column of malachite. Crimson cloth curtains hang before the tall doors, and keep the draught from the chilly East Indian.

'Is Mr. Trenchard at home?' asks Alexis, 'and can I see him on particular business?'

He has come to this house determined to keep no bounds—to exercise a husband's authority to the uttermost, if that stretch of power be needed—to claim his wife from his father's deadliest foe, Stephen Trenchard. Scarcely worth the claiming, perhaps, with that false blood in her veins. But some remnant of the old faithful love still lingers in his breast. If she will come back to him—if she will surrender all hope of her uncle's ill-gotten wealth, and come back to him, believing him still one of the humble toilers in life's great hive, he will take her back to his heart of hearts, and cherish her for all his life to come.

CHAPTER VIII.

BETWEEN LOVE AND GOLD.

THE footman surveys the stranger doubtfully, and rings a bell to summon Podmore the butler, feeling unequal to cope single-handed with this eruption of an unknown visitor at eight o'clock in the evening.

'Mr. Trenchard is not very well, sir. He is confined to his room, in fact; but if your business is anything important——'

Here Podmore comes to the subordinate's relief. He enters on the scene with a stately slowness, breathing heavily, having just been awakened from the pleasant slumber of repletion in front of the fire in the servants' hall, where buttered toast, eggs and ham, the daily papers, and a quiet game at cribbage are his evening solace.

'Mr. Trenchard is indisposed, sir,' he observes, severely, as if the stranger ought to have been aware of the fact; 'but if you wish I can carry him a

message.' The intruder looks like a gentleman, and
Podmore remembers that other mysterious visitor of
last summer, who came and went like the wind, no
one knowing whence or whither.   .

'If Miss Faunthorpe is at home and will see me,
I need not trouble Mr. Trenchard,' replies Alexis
after a moment's consideration.   'Be kind enough to
give her my card.'

Podmore stifles a yawn, and receives the card on a
salver, which he takes from the hall table, and
carries into the drawing-room, where Sibyl is sitting
in solitary grandeur dreaming over a volume of
Tennyson.

'A gentleman, ma'am, wishes to see Mr. Trenchard,
but I told him my master was indisposed. Would
you favour him with a few minutes' conversation,
ma'am?

'Is that the gentleman's card?' inquires Sibyl,
languidly.

'Yes, ma'am.'

Sibyl takes up the morsel of pasteboard with the
tips of her fingers, and that elegant air of listless-
ness which is so provoking to Marion. She looks at

the name a little curiously, notwithstanding her languor, for it strikes her suddenly that this visitor of to-night may be her uncle's mysterious guest of the race night. One glance at the card shows her the name of all others most appalling to her, and yet there is, in that first moment of surprise, a thrill of rapture in the thought that the one man she loves is near her.

'Where is he?' she cries, starting up from her easy chair with a display of animation that awakens Podmore's suspicious.

'In the 'all, ma'am. Shall I show him in?'

'Certainly.'

'How fortunate that uncle Trenchard should be out of the way to-night!' thinks Sibyl, too bewildered by the one startling fact of her husband's coming to be able to take in at a glance all the consequences of such an event.

Stephen Trenchard has been slightly ailing during the last week, and has kept himself hermetically sealed, as it were, against east winds in the seclusion of his bedchamber. He has suffered from such trifling indispositions, touches of cold and rheumatism, several times during the late autumn and early winter, and Mrs. Stormont is confirmed in her opinion that dear Mr. Trenchard is breaking fast, or, as the colonel puts it, in the friendly gossip across the walnuts and the wine, 'there can be no doubt the old fellow is going off the hooks.'

Podmore ushers Mr. Secretan into the drawing-room and retires, leaving husband and wife standing some yards apart, face to face.

Yes, there she stands. The wife lost so long, regretted so bitterly—there she stands, unchanged by care or sorrow, far lovelier than when he saw her last with the pinch of poverty on her cheek, and the wan pallor of care tarnishing the ivory whiteness of her complexion. She stands before him to-night the focus of all that is fairest in the luxurious room : amid all the upholsterer's gilding and colour she is the brightest spot. She is pale as marble, but the large dark eyes shine with a vivid light as she stretches out her hands to Alexis, as if in fondest welcome.

'Alex!' she cried, 'Alex! you have found me, in spite of all my care—found me too soon.'

She is ready to throw herself upon his breast and pour out her pent-up love in sobs and kisses, but his countenance does not invite this gush of feeling. He surveys her with a look in which there is more contempt than anger. 'Yes, I have found you,' he says; 'found you in the comfortable nest which you discovered for yourself when you turned your back upon starvation and me ;—found you in the house of my father's deadly enemy—of mine—for before I could speak plainly I had learned to hate him ;—yes, Mrs. Secretan, I have found you, and the clue to your mystery.'

'Alexis, you are too cruel. It was for your sake as much as for my own I came here. Yes, as Heaven hears and judges me, I thought of your happiness as much as of my own. Why should we both starve, when there was my uncle's fortune waiting for me to claim my share of it? I knew that he was an old man—that we could not have many years to wait.',

'And you left me to think you false, dishonoured, or dead, while you played out this paltry game of waiting for a dead man's shoes.'

'I spoke as plainly as I dared in my farewell letter. I was obliged to act secretly, knowing your prejudice against my uncle.'

'Don't give my sentiment so mild a name. It is hatred—or at best a sovereign contempt.'

'He has been so good to me, Alexis,' pleads Sibyl.

'No doubt. Vipers and scorpions and other noxious reptiles are kindly to their offspring, I dare say. You are of his own treacherous blood. There is sympathy between you.'

'Alexis, how can you be so cruel? Did you come here only to torture me?'

'I came here to discover whether you are my wife or no. I came to offer you your choice between Mr. Trenchard's fortune—a fortune founded on treachery, remember—and my love. I am ready to forgive all I have suffered at your hands,—your desertion of me in my bitterest need, my suspense and pain of these three years past—if you will place your hand in mine to-night, and leave this hateful house, and abandon all hope of profiting by its master's bounty.'

'**And my uncle is dying,** perhaps,' Sibyl thinks despairingly. '**In a few weeks I** might inherit **his fortune.**'

'The choice is simple,' says Alexis. '**You cannot** have much difficulty in deciding either way. **On one side your uncle's** garnered wealth, a million perhaps, there is no limit to the opportunities **of a man** who begins unscrupulously. On the other side **my** affection, a husband you once pretended **to** love——'

'**Pretended!** Oh, Alexis, what more real than **my love?** When have I ever **ceased to love** you? If **you could** only know——'

'**I know** nothing except that after **three** years' **severance I find you** here, my enemy's adopted **daughter, the centre** of all those fine things which women **of** small minds value. I ask you, as many a man has asked **many a woman** before to-day, to leave all unreservedly for my sake. I do not ask you **to return to** starvation remember, or to the **genteel** adventurer's hand-to-mouth existence. **I** have learned to earn my daily bread. The pinch **of poverty** need touch **you no more.**'

'Not till health fails you, or we grow old,' returns Sibyl. 'I know what the workers for their daily bread have to look forward to when that day comes. The workhouse or the river. Alexis, for pity's sake, be reasonable. If my uncle Trenchard's fortune was founded on money that ought to have been your father's—he makes the story tell against your father, mind—so much the more reason that it should come to you and me when he is dead. He is past seventy, and his health has been failing during the last few months. He cannot live much longer, and I am as certain as I can be of anything that he means to leave me the bulk of his fortune. Why should I throw away such a chance?'

'Simply because money so obtained would be odious to me, as it should be to you. You are as false to Stephen Trenchard as you have been to me. Your presence in this house is a fraud. Do you think your uncle would leave his money to the wife of Philip Secretan's son?'

'Perhaps not,' falters Sibyl. 'But for his money to come back to you would be an act of restitution. Providence works in that way sometimes.'

'Providence **never** works through lies and hypo-crisies. I want' **none of** Stephen Trenchard's money; **all of it tainted** with **fraud** and lying, **I'll warrant. I want you,** the penniless girl I married four years **ago. I** had no thought of a fortune when I asked **you to be** my wife, Sibyl. I have no thought of a fortune now.'

' No, Alex. **You** were always reckless, and your recklessness brought us to the threshold of starvation, and would bring **us there** again, no doubt, if **I let** you have your way.'

' That means you are not coming with **me.** You hold by **your** rich uncle in preference **to** your **husband.'**

'**Alex,** I love you with **all my heart. You are never** absent **from my thoughts ;** the hope of **our** reunion is the one hope that brightens my life.'

'**I will** believe that if you put your hand in mine **and say, "I am yours,** husband, come weal **or** woe." I might **claim** you, **by** law, remember—claim **you as my chattel.** But I am too proud to do that. You must follow me freely or **not at all You** shall **have** your choice.'

'In a few months my uncle may be dead. I will come to you then.'

'I will not have you then, neither you nor your ill-gotten wealth. Revel in it, fatten on it, but you shall be no wife of mine unless you leave this house with me to-night.'

'It would be too great a folly to abandon every chance when success seems so near.'

'You decide for the rich uncle?'

'Alex!' cries Sibyl, wringing her hands, 'how can you be so cruel to me? Can't you understand that it is for your sake as much as for my own that I want to be rich?'

'I cannot, for I have told you plainly that I despise wealth so won. I see you have made your choice, and I have now only one thing more to settle before I leave you to the fulfilment of your destiny. What have you done with our child?'

'He is in safe keeping.'

'I can believe that, but it is not quite enough. I want the custody of him.'

'How could you take care of so young a child— a toy of scarcely three years old?'

' I would take excellent care of him.'

' He would be a burden **to** you.'

' I should **not** think him **a burden.**'

' Alexis !' exclaimed Sibyl, bursting into **tears,** ' I have deceived you. I did not like **to** tell **you the truth. Our boy** is dead. He died within **a week of his birth.'**

' Heartless woman ! you have fooled me **with a** false hope. I have built all my schemes of future happiness upon that child, **and** now you tell me **he is** dead. Which am I to believe, your letter or your assertion of his death ? '

' **I** have .**no motive for** deceiving **you** in **this matter.** You offer to take the charge of him off my **hands. If** he lived I should be glad **to** accept such **an offer.'**

' Perhaps, for you who **have** so little **of** a wife's affection cannot have much of the maternal instinct.'

' Alexis !' she cries, despairingly.

She runs to him and throws herself into his arms, and sobs upon his breast, distracted between love and ambition. The glittering prize seems too **near for her to let it go.** She cannot bring herself to say farewell fortune, welcome love. She clings to her husband as if she could not part with him, yet means all the while to be steadfast in her devotion to Stephen Trenchard and his money.

'Alexis, if you would only be patient! Let me stay with my uncle to the end. It is not far off. Every one tells me he has not long to live. Trust in my devotion to you, my fidelity.'

'Yes, trust in your devotion, your fidelity, while the town gossips are busy with the rumour of your approaching marriage with Sir Wilford Cardonnel.'

'The merest folly. Sir Wilford has done me the honour to admire me, and my uncle has given him some little encouragement. You have nothing to fear from such a rival, Alexis, or from any rival. My heart belongs to you. My love has never wavered.'

'And as a proof of this unwavering love you refuse to leave this house, all this crimson satin and gilding, for the humble home which I can offer you.'

'I refuse to throw away a fortune which only a lunatic would consent to sacrifice,' replies Sibyl, with a touch of impatience.

The worthy Podmore enters at this juncture to replenish the fire. He approaches the hearth with slow and ponderous steps, taking note of all he sees on his passage, Sibyl's agitated, tear-stained face, her visitor's pale and angry looks.

'Good-bye, Miss Faunthorpe,' says Alexis, while the butler is doctoring the fire with deliberate care, as if every flame were a precious life in danger of extinction. 'I think I've explained all I wish you to convey to your uncle.'

' Yes,' she falters.

'Good night.'

'Good night. Are you going to leave Redcastle soon ? '

' By the first train to-morrow morning.

' Good-bye.'

She would give much to say more—to entreat him once again to be patient and to look forward to their reunion later—to accept her by-and-bye, burdened with the weight of Stephen Trenchard's wealth. But the astute Podmore, having heard the note of leave-taking, waits to show the visitor out, and Alexis is presently escorted to the hall door as if by the warder of a prison.

He goes out of that house well-nigh heart-broken, though pride has enabled him to bear himself quietly enough, and even to make light of his disappointment.

'I loved her so well that it is hard to find her worthless,' he tells himself. 'Not one spark of generous feeling—all sordid greed of gain. Had I told her of my altered fortunes she would have come to me. Yes, she might, perhaps, have surrendered Stephen Trenchard's larger wealth. But I thank God I had resolution enough to keep that secret. And so good-bye, my dream of domestic life, my hope of an heir to inherit my name. I stand alone henceforth, wifeless with a wife, childless though a child has been born to me, whose baby face I was not permitted to see.'

CHAPTER IX.

WHEN her husband is gone, and the full significance of that meeting and parting comes home to her, Sibyl feels as if all the hope and glory of her life were departed with him. She does not repent her decision. Were Alexis to offer her the same choice again she would decide in exactly the same manner. In her limited way of looking at the question there is no possibility of arriving at any other determination. It would seem to her utterly unreasonable, an act of absolute lunacy to throw away a fortune which is ready to drop into her lap, for which she has waited patiently, living her false life, suppressing the truer instincts of her heart and mind for nearly three years. She wonders that a man of the world can demand such a sacrifice, can cling to so foolish a prejudice as hereditary hatred, and even carry that passion so

far as to hate his enemy's money. To her mind
the inheritance of Stephen Trenchard's fortune by
Alexis Secretan's wife appears a wise and bene-
ficent settlement of an old debt. No doubt her
uncle Stephen was right, and that Philip Secretan
was a spendthrift who deserved to be disinherited.
His father's fortune held over, quadrupled, increased
tenfold perhaps, in Stephen's prudent hands, would
pass to Alexis, and justice would be done to the
dead father through the living son.

Sibyl cannot believe that Alexis will be obdurate when the hour of her freedom comes with
Stephen Trenchard's death.

'No, I will not despair,' she says to herself,
drying her tearful eyes, and looking at her white
face in the glass over the low marble chimney-
piece. 'Cruel as he was to-night, he loves me too
well to repudiate me by-and-bye when I am free
to return to him. Poor fellow! How could he
reject fortune if it were mine to give him; he,
who has suffered the sharp stings of poverty, and
who has to work for his daily bread? How could
he turn his back upon the bright new life that

would lie before us if my uncle's money were
mine—not life within the four walls of a handsome dungeon, like this house, but life wherever
earth is loveliest—in Paris, in Italy, sailing in our
yacht on the Mediterranean, free as birds, without
a care or a thought except how to get the most
pleasure out of our youth and wealth and
freedom?'

Comforted by reflections like these, Sibyl calms
herself, and prepares to continue her part of min-
istering angel to Stephen Trenchard. Illness
makes the old man irritable, and the character is
not the easiest in the world to perform.

She trembles at the thought of what would
happen if her uncle and her husband were to
meet—of what might have happened this very
evening but for Mr. Trenchard's most fortunate
indisposition. What limit would there be to the
old man's fury if he were to discover that he had
been cheated of his affection—that the niece he
had loved and favoured was the wife of his enemy's
son? That revelation would have destroyed her
hopes, beggared her of that golden chance which

seems to her scarcely less than the actual possession
of his fortune.

She has no easy part to play this evening
when she goes up to her uncle's room, and finds
him sitting by his fire awake and watchful—the
Times lying uncut on the little table beside his
capacious arm-chair.

'What have you been doing all the evening,
child?' he asks testily. 'I've been waiting for
you to read me the City article—waiting upwards
of an hour by that clock,' he adds, with a glance at
the gilded timepiece on the mantel shelf.

'I'm so sorry, dear uncle. I thought you were
asleep.'

'You might have taken the trouble to come
and ascertain the fact. I have not closed my eyes
since Podmore brought me my beef tea. Who
is this gentleman, pray, who has detained you so
long?'

Sibyl is unprepared for this question. She had
hoped her uncle would have known nothing about
that untimely visitor.

'A gentleman uncle,?'

'Yes. Podmore **told me** you had a gentleman with you. Some one who wanted to see me on particular business, and, **being told that I was** ill, asked **to see** you instead. What did **the fellow** want?'

'**He** wanted you to subscribe to a fund for building a **new church at** Krampston, uncle,' replies Sibyl, with a desperate plunge. **Some lie she must** needs invent, no matter what shape it took. 'Some **new sect, if** I understood him rightly. I told him **I did not think** you would **care to** subscribe, **but that he might call again, if he** liked, when **you are well.'**

'Humph! **You might** have given him **a de-**cided negative **at once.** There are churches enough **in the world,** and new sects enough, without **my** squandering money on the fools who want more. **The fellow** was with you a long time. Why couldn't **you get rid** of him sooner?'

'**He insisted** upon showing me plans, and **a** list of subscribers, and he told me a good deal about the church.'

'You ought to know how to keep such fellows

at a distance. Some swindler, no doubt. And he was with you nearly an hour, according to Podmore.'

'Shall I read you the City article, uncle Trenchard ?' asks Sibyl, anxious to end this embarrassing discussion.

She seats herself a little way behind Mr. Trenchard's chair, well in the shadow.

'Yes, you can read, but come nearer the lamp, child ; it makes me uncomfortable to know that you are straining your eyes in the dark there.'

Sibyl obeys reluctantly, fearing that the traces of agitation may still disfigure her countenance. Luckily, the lamp has a velvet shade which casts the light on the paper in her hand, and not on the face bending over it.

Mr. Trenchard scans her curiously, notwithstanding. His suspicions have been aroused by that evening visitor—a handsome young man, according to Podmore, a lover, perhaps, and that story of the Krampston Church all a fable. Mr. Trenchard has employed too much fiction in the course of his own career to be easily deluded by a figment of the female brain.

He says nothing, however, content to suspect, and to keep his suspicions to himself for the present.

He languishes for some days more under the burden of what Dr. Mitsand calls a slight bronchial attack, and in about a week is able to come downstairs again, and seems almost as active and alert as ever, Sibyl thinks, wondering whether there is really any foundation for that idea about his 'breaking up.'

Dr. Mitsand is Mr. Trenchard's medical attendant. It is not to be supposed that the precious life of a millionaire could be trusted to poor little Dr. Faunthorpe, who has the care of the parish, and goes his rounds in a positively disreputable pony carriage. Dr. Mitsand's neat single brougham and fine pair of bay cobs are a standing evidence of his respectability and his skill. If he were not a clever doctor how could he afford those cobs ?

' Wonderful constitution, your uncle's, Miss Faunthorpe,' says Dr. Mitsand, cheerily, on the occasion of his last professional visit. " Quite set up again, you see, complexion clearer, eye brighter, liver in better order. I congratulate you upon having an uncle who ought to live as long as Lyndhurst or Brougham."

Sibyl tries to look glad, but her heart sinks at the thought that this fine constitution of her uncle's places the hope of reunion with Alexis very far off.

'What a miserable situation mine must be when such horrid thoughts are forced upon me!' she reflects. 'I almost wish I were Marion, dawdling away life in that old house at the bottom of the town, without a care.'

Sibyl's cares are rendered heavier just at this time by the marked attentions of Sir Wilford Cardonnel, attentions which, however delightful they might be to her vanity in the beginning of things, have now become hateful to her, the more so as her uncle will not allow her any way of escape from this entanglement. She sees before her the inevitable end in a proposal from Sir Wilford, and her rejection of it, which act of seeming

idiocy will doubtless provoke her uncle's anger,
perhaps forfeit his good graces for ever; and then
all her patience, all her pretty little flatteries and
gentle ministerings to an irritable old man will
have been wasted.   She will have grieved and
offended her husband, perhaps alienated his affec-
tions—for nothing.   She will be bankrupt both
ways.   These possibilities occur to her mind sometimes.   Difficulties crowd upon her and hem her
in on every side.   The dread of Sir Wilford taking
that decisive step, which he evidently intends to
take sooner or later, is always before her; and
she has another ever-present fear in the thought
that Alexis may reappear at any moment, and
reveal himself to Stephen Trenchard.   There are
hours of her life in which she feels sorely tempted
to run away from wealth as she ran away from
poverty; and it is possible that if she had known
where to find her husband she would have acted
upon this impulse.   But he has vanished out of
her existence.   In the fear and confusion of that
brief visit of his she did not even ask his place of
abode or mode of life.

Prudence and that deep-rooted worship of wealth which is sometimes engendered by a long apprenticeship to poverty keeps Sibyl constant to the rack of her daily difficulties, despite these occasional longings for escape. She contrives by a certain distance of manner, which is in no wise ungracious, to defer Sir Wilford's declaration of his passion. The bluff and genial baronet is as shy as a girl in the presence of the woman he loves, and so long as he can enjoy Sibyl's society, is in no hurry to precipitate matters. Small as are the tokens of favour which she has bestowed upon him, Sir Wilford has no apprehension of being refused by her when it shall please him to ask the fateful question. He is too good a match for the possibility of a refusal. It does not enter into his notion of possibilities that he, Sir Wilford Cardonnel, of The How, could be rejected by any woman out of the peerage. He is kept at a distance by Sibyl's coldness, but in no wise disheartened.

'I'm in no hurry, you know,' he says to himself. 'I like to know something about a woman before I ask her to be my wife. I should like to make sure she cared a little about me, in a quiet way. So many women have thrown themselves at my head, that I like this one all the better for not going so fast. More likely to be a good stayer, I should think. I don't want to win with a rush. I'd rather take my time and come in quietly.' Thus muses Sir Wilford in the solitude of his study —a room chiefly devoted to treatises on the turf and farriery, whips, single sticks, gloves, favourite bits and bridles, a small menagerie of stuffed dogs, from Sebastian, the favourite old hound, defunct at a ripe old age, blind of one eye, and short of one ear, to Mite, the smallest terrier ever seen in the West Riding, a minute white animal, with pointed pink paws and a strong likeness to a rat.

'I ought to see more of her,' thinks Sir Wilford. 'It's no use asking her and the old party to dinner, or dining with them. I shall never make the running that way. I feel as strange with her when I haven't seen her for a week or two as if I'd only just been introduced to her. It's like beginning our acquaintance over again. I must make Phœbe ask them here to stay. That 'll be the best plan. A week in the same house with her will show me what kind of girl she is, better than a twelvemonth's morning calling and dining.'

And having made up his mind, Sir Wilford is not slow to act upon his decision.

' Hi, Jess, old lady,' he calls to his favourite, a splendid red setter, graceful and ladylike enough in her habits to be admitted as a house dog, though not without protest from Phœbe. Jess vanquishes Miss Cardonnel's objections by pretending to adore her, is as artful as a court favourite, and has as many perquisites.

Sir Wilford goes straight to the morning-room, where his two sisters employ themselves industriously between breakfast and luncheon, writing innumerable letters, examining the housekeeper's weekly accounts, the head gardener's book, and other household volumes, working point lace, practising classical sonatas which reduce them to the verge of lunacy, and making winter clothing for their various pensioners.

Christmas is just over, and the Christmas gaieties and benevolences done with. It is the beginning of the New Year—fine healthy weather—the ground not too hard for horses or hounds, and Sir Wilford in good humour with the arrangement of things.

'Well, Phœbe, what people are you going to ask for Tilberry steeplechase?' he inquires, as Miss Cardonnel looks up from her desk, where she is just declaring herself to remain her dearest Cecilia's ever affectionate friend—Cecilia being the fifth dearest friend she has addressed this morning.

Tilberry steeplechase is an important fixture in this part of the world. It is a race at which gentlemen jockeys disport themselves. It comes in the winter, when outdoor amusements are rare. Altogether Tilberry steeplechase is a benefaction.

'I've written the last of my invitations this morning,' replies Phœbe, who is somewhat inclined to forget that she is the prime minister and not the king, and to commit herself to important measures without the preliminary formula of consultation with her sovereign. 'I have asked General and Mrs. McTower and Belinda—the eldest, you know;—and I thought we ought to be civil to the Vicar of Redcastle for once in a way, so I've asked Mr. and Mrs.

Chasubel and the son.   He won't make much difference, and you can put him in the barracks.'

The barracks is a range of small bedrooms over the
offices, devoted to bachelor visitors of indistinction.

'Very well; I've no objection to the Chasubels.
Who else ? '

'The Radnors, and the Vernons, and Cecilia
Hawtree.'

'Too many women,' says Sir Wilford.

'Cecilia is my particular friend,' remarks Miss
Cardonnel, with dignity.

' Oh, well, let her come.'

'She is coming the day after to-morrow,' observes Miss Cardonnel.   'I have just written to say
I shall send the omnibus to meet her.'

'What the dooce can one young woman want
with a family bus, built to carry ten ?' exclaims Sir
Wilford.

'She will have her maid,' replies Miss Cardonnel,
'and her portmanteaux.'

'Ah, boxes enough to load a goods train, I dare
say,' mutters Sir Wilford.   'Well, that's all your
list, I suppose ?'

'Yes, Wilford.'

'Then I'll give you mine.'

'Do you want to ask any one else?' exclaims Miss Cardonnel, with an injured air. 'I fancied I had thought of every one you would have cared about asking.'

'You've thought of a good many I don't care about.'

'But, my dear Wilford, I don't see how I can possibly ask any more. I've filled all the best bed-rooms.'

'Then you must empty some of them. I want you to ask Colonel and Mrs. Stormont, and that son of their's on the gray.'

'But, Wilford, Mrs. Stormont is such a horrid old person—so pushing.'

'Never mind that. We often have horrid old persons.'

'And the son,—I don't know what he's like off that gray, but he's utterly odious on it.'

'Stupid young cad, rather, but good fun. Be sure you tell him to bring the gray.'

'Why should we have the Stormonts to stay

with us, Wilford?' demands Lavinia, the younger
sister, looking up from an easel, upon which she has
been copying a drawing-master's landscape, and
fondly deluding herself with the idea that she can
paint. 'It's all very well to ask them to dinner
once in a way, or to a garden party, but why have
them in the house?'

'Simply because I wish it, Vinnie. I don't
often indulge in whims. Say that this is one, if
you like.'

'Oh, of course, if you really wish it. But I
think it's rather a dangerous precedent,' replies
Phœbe. 'All the Redcastle people will be expecting to be asked to stay here.'

'The butchers and bakers and candlestick-
makers. Well, they can go down to their graves in
a state of expectation,' says Sir Wilford, 'and now
Phœbe, I want you to write a particularly nice letter
—cordial, and all that kind of thing, you know—to
Miss Faunthorpe, asking her and Mr. Trenchard
over for the race week.'

'I ought to have known what was coming,' exclaims Phœbe.

'Well, naturally, I shouldn't be civil to the Stormonts without a motive. Mrs. Stormont introduced me to Miss Faunthorpe, you see, and I shouldn't like the old lady to think I'd make a cat's-paw of her.'

Phœbe is inwardly rebellious, but too wise to revolt outwardly. She has seen the sun set on her twenty-ninth birthday, and has been mistress of the How, the sole and sovereign domestic power, for the last ten years. It will be a hard thing, to lay down her sceptre, to retire from that lordly dwelling-place, and to become Miss Cardonnel of nowhere in particular, a young lady whose non-success in the matrimonial line sympathizing friends will lament over. And Phœbe feels that the day when her sceptre must be so resigned is not very far off, now that Wilford, who has his father's obstinate temper, poor dear fellow, has taken a ridiculous fancy to this Miss Faunthorpe, a mere nobody, with nothing but a pretty face and a rich uncle to recommend her to notice.

Sir Wilford waits while his sister writes the letter of invitation, which she is obliged to make much warmer in tone than inclination would prompt; the baronet looking over her shoulder all the while.

When the letter is in its envelope he surprises Phœbe by taking it from her and putting it in his pocket.

'I am going over to Redcastle this afternoon,' he says, 'so I can deliver the letter and bring you back an answer. I should like you to give Miss Faunthorpe the tapestry room.'

'My dear Wilford, what are you thinking of? I have ever so many married couples coming.. I must put her in one of the small rooms in the Kneller gallery.'

'Oh, very well,' replies Sir Wilford, 'she'll have the pick of the rooms, perhaps, some of these days. —Hi, Jess, old woman.'

With which awful threat Sir Wilford withdraws, leaving his sisters free to discuss the calamity that lowers over their house.

CHAPTER X.

MARION IS RAISED TO DISTINCTION.

SIR WILFORD, clad in the latest fashion in checks, a rough and fleecy raiment which his father would have deemed better suited to clothe his gamekeeper or groom than himself, and mounted on Bull of Bashan, is a sight to behold this winter afternoon as he trots gaily down the wide avenue at the How, and emerges therefrom on a bold and open country. The Bull is a little fresh this afternoon, which, being interpreted, means that the grooms have been too lazy to take the superfluous energy out of that amiable animal for the last two days, whereby the Bull behaves like a quadruped newly introduced to a strange country, where all sights and sounds, colours and shapes of objects, lights and shadows, are new to him. He shies ferociously at every trunk in the long line of elms, and indulges in a serpentine movement for the length of the avenue. He

takes objection to the colour of the gravel where the
road has been mended; and on suddenly beholding
the white gate, which he ought to know as well as
his own manger, recoils on his haunches, and curls
himself up into a ball, and in this shape canters
furiously into the road, startling the lazy waggoner
asleep upon his wain, and rousing a flight of rooks
from their afternoon repose by the clatter of his iron
shoes. The cawing of the rooks finishes the Bull
altogether, and sends him off like a maniac, or de-
moniacally possessed animal; but Sir Wilford having
now got him into the open country is able to 'take
it out of him' over a fine stretch of moorland, and
brings him back to the high road a couple of miles
further off, a subdued and subjugated beast, willing
to settle into a comfortable trot, which, with an occasional interval of walking, carries Sir Wilford into
Redcastle by afternoon tea-time, that pleasant hour
betwixt day and night, when labour rests, or should
rest, from its cares, and the household music of the
kettle singing on the hob speaks peace to the soul of
the weary.

Mr. Trenchard is taking afternoon tea with his

two nieces, Sibyl and Marion, in the firelit drawing-
room at Lancaster Lodge, a room which, like most
other rooms, looks its best by that uncertain light,
now gorgeous in the glow of crimson and gold, anon
wrapped in shadow.   Marion has been invited to
spend the day; the two girls have employed the
short winter afternoon in a review of Sibyl's last
new dresses, an inspection which has not been con-
ducive to the younger sister's peace of mind or good
temper.

At the announcement of Sir Wilford Cardonnel
however, Marion brightens a little, and is glad.

'How lucky he should have called to-day!' she
thinks. 'Sibyl is too mean to ask me here on purpose
to see him, and now he must be introduced to me
and I can talk about knowing him as well as Sibyl.
What will Maria Harrison say, I wonder, when I
tell her that I am quite intimate with Sir Wilford
Cardonnel?'

Marion little knows the mighty honour which
fate has reserved for her—little dreams that by the
happy accident of her presence at Lancaster Lodge
this afternoon she is to be raised to a giddy height

of grandeur, from which she will hardly be able to glance downwards without vertigo.

Sir Wilford is presented to Miss Marion Faunthorpe in due form by Mr. Trenchard, and the conversation becomes at once general and sprightly, glancing upon such original topics as the probability of a hard frost before long, the advantage of the present weather from a sporting point of view, the health and well-being of the baronet's stud, the superlative virtues and capabilities of his latest equine purchase, the probability of a day's good racing at Tilberry.

'You ought to see Tilberry steeplechase,' says Sir Wilford. 'Tilberry Common's only three miles from the How, you know, and it's an uncommonly good day's sport, gentlemen jocks, and that kind of thing. I've ridden there myself, but I didn't enter anything this year. You ought really, you know, Miss Faunthorpe; in point of fact, I came over here this afternoon on purpose to ask you and Mr. Trenchard to come and stay with us next week. My sister gave me a letter for you. She's dreadfully anxious for you to come, and I think the change of air would do **Mr.** Trenchard **good.** We stand a good bit higher than you do, you know, and get **a** sniff **off** the moors,—remarkably healthy, **that kind of** thing, I'm **told. Do** say **yes now, Mr.** Trenchard,' he urges, handing Sibyl the letter.

'I'm afraid my dear uncle's health won't **permit him to** leave home,' answers Sibyl. '**He** has been quite **an** invalid lately, you know, Sir Wilford.'

'All the more reason he should have change of air—brace him up, **you know.** Capital **thing** for invalids, moorland air. And if Miss Mary Ann——'

'Marion,' interjects that young lady. Not even by Sir Wilford **Cardonnel will she** submit **to** be called Mary Ann.

'If Miss Miriam——'

'Marion.'

I beg your pardon, **I'm shaw.** If Miss Marion will come I shall be delighted, and I'm sure my sister will be quite awfully **glad.**'

Marion blushes crimson **with delight at** such an invitation.

'You're too kind,' she gasps. '**I** positively doat upon races.'

'I shouldn't have thought your passion for them had had time to reach such a height,' says Sibyl, sneeringly, 'since you never were at a race in your life before last year's summer meeting.'

She is provoked at Marion's eagerness to accept an invitation, the acceptance of which can only bring embarrassment upon her, Sibyl.

'That means you'll come,' exclaims Sir Wilford, answering Marion, 'and, of course, if you say yes, Miss Faunthorpe can't say no. Sisters always think alike—two cherries on one stalk, like Juno's swans, together and inseparable, you know; and now we only want Mr. Trenchard's acquiescence.'

'I should be a churl to refuse so hospitable an invitation, and to deprive these girls of so much pleasure,' replies Stephen Trenchard.

'Bravo!' cries Sir Wilford; 'then it's all settled. You'll come next Saturday?'

'I don't think I could be ready by Saturday,' murmurs Marion, with an awful fear upon the subject of her wardrobe, which will need herculean labours of cutting and contriving, and some expenditure of cash, before it can be fit for the halls of Cardonnel.

'Pray, dear uncle, do not think of us,' says Sibyl, 'I don't at all care about races, and, much as I appreciate Miss Cardonnel's kind invitation, I really would rather not accept it, for fear the fatigue and the excitement should be too much for you.'

'Nasty thing,' thinks Marion, 'she refuses just because I'm invited.'

'Artful puss,' thinks Stephen, 'she keeps him on by holding him off.'

'Don't be afraid about your uncle, Miss Faunthorpe,' says Sir Wilford, 'we shall be awfully careful of him.'

'I'm not quite so decrepid as my niece thinks me,' says Mr. Trenchard, 'and I shall quite enjoy a few days at the How.'

'That's glorious,' cries Sir Wilford. 'On Saturday, then. You'll drive over in time for luncheon? Be sure you bring your habit, Miss Faunthorpe. I've a chestnut mare that will suit you to perfection. And I can mount you too, Miss Marion, if you like riding?'

'I positively adore it,' gushes Marion. 'Sibyl and I used to take it in turns to ride uncle Robert's

pony when we were little things. I was so sorry
when the pony grew too small for us.'

Sir Wilford, having settled this important
question, and drunk three cups of tea, chiefly for
the pleasure of having his cup and saucer handed
him by Sibyl, departs, leaving the elder sister heavy-
hearted, the younger in a state of wild excitement,
which her natural awe of Stephen Trenchard can
hardly subdue.

'What am I to do about my things, Sibyl?'
she whispers, as the two girls sit side by side on a
sofa by the fire.

'What things?'

'My dresses, jackets, gloves, hats, boots, everything.
I've hardly a rag that's fit to wear at the How.'

'Then you oughtn't to have accepted the invitation. You might have seen that you were only
asked because you happened to be here, and Sir
Wilford could not very well leave you out.'

'How unkind of you to say that!'

'It's preposterous to accept an invitation when
you have no clothes fit to be worn at the house
you're asked to visit. You ought to have refused.'

'Ought I ? That's very nice and sisterly of you, I'm sure. Very much like twin cherries and Juno's fiddlesticks. Just the only chance I ever had of enjoying myself and seeing life,—going into society, in fact, and a chance that would give me quite a new position in Redcastle, bring those horrid Stormonts and that disgusting Mrs. Groshen to their senses; and you expect me to refuse it. It's positively unnatural of you, Sibyl.' And Marion relieves her bursting heart with a gush of tears.

'Why, what's the matter, girl ?' cries Stephen Trenchard, starting from that placid slumber into which the fire-glow and the subdued murmur of the girls' voices have beguiled him. 'You don't come here to cry, I hope, Marion. If we make you unhappy you'd better stay away.'

Mr. Trenchard is not the kind of man to allow his afternoon repose to be disturbed by a whimpering niece. His young kinsfolk must make themselves agreeable if they hope to retain his favour.

It's all Sibyl's unkindness,' says Marion, swallowing her sobs in an unpleasantly convulsive manner. 'She hasn't a bit of heart, she never had.

When Sir Wilford Cardonnel has invited me and all, she throws my poverty in my face, and says I must refuse the invitation on account of my things.'

'What does the girl mean by things?'

'I simply reminded Marion that the invitation gives us very short notice, and that her wardrobe is hardly fit for visiting at the How.'

'Oh, is that all?' exclaims Mr. Trenchard. 'That shan't stand in your way, Marion. You can get whatever you want for this visit at Carmichael's, and have it put down to Sibyl's account.'

'Oh, uncle, you are too good, too generous,' gasps Marion, forgetting how often she has inveighed against Mr. Trenchard's meanness.

'Don't make a fuss, please, Marion,' says Stephen, closing his eyes again.

Sibyl is gloomy. She would do much to prevent this visit, were there any way open to her by which it could be prevented. She feels that to visit at Sir Wilford's house is a kind of treason against her husband. True that the baronet is not yet her declared admirer, but his admiration is not the less obvious, and the town gossips have already

been busy with her name and Sir Wilford's. How
provoking uncle Trenchard is—and Marion too!
She hates them both, and preserves a sullen manner
towards Marion all the evening, a sullenness which
that young lady imputes to jealousy.

'Perhaps she thinks that Sir Wilford might be
fickle enough to admire me a little,' muses Marion,
elated beyond measure by the prospect of her visit,
and the idea of getting 'things' at Carmichael's.
'Of course Sibyl is the beauty, we all know that;
but I flatter myself I have a little more animation
than she has, and in the long run, fascinating manners are more admired than good looks.'

Fortified thus in her self-esteem Marion departs
in the highest spirits, after having made Sibyl
promise to go shopping with her next morning.

Sibyl makes her preparations for the visit with a
heavy heart. She assists Marion kindly enough
now that she has resigned herself to the inevitable.
She lends her sister the aid of her counsel, and considerably chastens Marion's taste in colours and
patterns, a taste which inclines to the 'loud' and
'fast,' large checks, big metal buttons, yachting

jackets, and small pork-pie hats. Sibyl takes care that her sister shall be dressed like a lady, which may be done cheaply, and not like a fashion plate, the latter involving lavish expenditure, and often resulting in disappointment. Sibyl selects hues which harmonize with Marion's hair and complexion, and not the last new colour, which the shopman presses upon her, as if novelty and beauty were convertible terms.

'I'm afraid you'll make me an awful dowdy,' remonstrates Marion, who is inclined to object to the combination of rich brown and soft cream-colour, which Sibyl recommends for a walking costume, and this languid shade of blue, relieved by ruchings, pipings, and flouncings of palest salmon, which Sibyl declares will make a lovely dinner dress.

'See what Miss Eylett will say to my choice,' says Sibyl.

'Oh, of course that old Eylett will side with you. She knows how to flatter a good customer.'

'Choose for yourself then, Marion, and be happy.'

'Well, upon my word, I don't know what to

have,' says Marion, surveying the counter, and biting the tip of her gloved forefinger to assist cogitation 'There's that lovely peach. I should like of all things, and that heavenly maize. Think of it trimmed with black lace.'

'Charming for a brunette, but odious for a blonde. And to trim it properly you would want at least fifty pounds' worth of lace.'

'That apple-green brocade, then, with the lovely rosebuds.'

'Admirable for a dowager, but quite unsuited to you.'

'I wonder if uncle Trenchard would mind my having a ruby velvet? I have always fancied a ruby velvet.'

'With a diamond tiara, of course. Most appropriate for a country surgeon's niece, especially when he's the parish doctor.'

'Well, I suppose you'd better choose. I'll have the blue and salmon, but it's a horrid thin silk.'

'Quite good enough for an evening dress, which will be done for when its freshness is gone.'

So Marion finally accepts Sibyl's superior judg-

ment. Her purchases include a pretty gray merino
for mornings and walking, a rich brown silk, the pale
blue dinner dress, and a handsome black cloth jacket,
garments which are judiciously bought for something
less than thirty pounds. With these materials the
two girls drive straight to Miss Eylett, who, with
much persuasion from Sibyl, is induced to promise
the three dresses for Saturday morning.

'And now all you have to do is to get Hester to
wash and iron your white muslins,' says Sibyl, 'so
that you may have some simple dresses for the
quiet evenings. I'll lend you a sash or two.'

'Upon my word, Sib, you're quite a darling.
What made you so disagreeable last night?'

'I don't want to go to the How, and I was vexed
with you and uncle Trenchard for snapping at the
invitation.'

'Don't want to go to the How!' cries Marion,
with as much astonishment as if Sibyl had said she
didn't wish to go to heaven. 'Don't want to go to
the How, when it's the grandest chance you ever had
in your life, and people are beginning to say that you
can be Lady Cardonnel if you like.'

'People are idiots and busybodies. I don't want to be Lady Cardonnel, or Lady anybody else.'

'Sibyl, don't be so affected!' exclaims Marion, disgusted by a repudiation which she believes thoroughly insincere.

Mr. Trenchard's carriage deposits Marion at the shabby old house beyond the minster, and Jenny comes rushing out into the wintry air—last year's tartan frock a good deal too short for those obtrusive legs of hers—to kiss Sibyl, to the disgust of the coachman, who looks upon this branch of his employer's family as a low lot.

'That's tne worst of living with these here novvo riches,' he complains to John the footman. 'They may climb the ladder of fortune theirselves, but they leave their relations a-grovellin' at the bottom.'

'What do you mean by novvo riches?' inquires the simple John.

'Well, parwennoos, stoopid, if you must 'av the wernackerler.'

Hester and Jenny Faunthorpe have rather a hard time of it for the rest of this important week, Hester at the wash-tub and the ironing-board, Jane engaged in darning stockings and sewing on tapes and buttons, her sister's wardrobe requiring more small repairs than are consistent with a notion of order and industry in its owner.

'Well, you have let your things go to seed, Marion,' remarks Jane. 'If it hadn't been for this visit of yours I should think you must have dropped to pieces altogether before long.'

'You're an impertinent chit,' exclaims Marion, frowning over a complicated darn.

'Well, you might be civil when I'm toiling like a slave for you.'

'You may help me or leave it alone, just as you please. It's no pleasure to be under an obligation to you.'

'As far as inclination goes, I'd much rather leave it alone,' replies the argumentative Jane, 'but for the credit of the family I shall do my best to prevent you going into society with your heels coming through your stockings. But I can't help saying that I think you'd find it better for the health of your stockings to darn them before they come to this;' and Jenny emphasizes her remark by thrusting her hand through a yawning chasm in the stocking she is operating upon.

‘ Keep your opinions to yourself, and don't make the holes bigger by sticking your enormous hand through them,’ says Marion.

‘ This is a grateful world,’ murmurs Jane, re-signedly.

Dr. Faunthorpe is pleased at the idea of his younger niece's pleasure, though the visit to the How will drag a pound or two out of his scantily furnished purse, pounds already engaged for tax or water rate, as the case may be, and the subtraction of which will throw his financial arrangements out of gear for ever so long. But Robert Faunthorpe is one of those good little men whose mission upon this earth seems to be to suffer and be patient, if not to suffer and be strong. Nay, is there not exceeding strength in this quiet patience, this placid endurance of loss and deprivation, this uncomplaining surrender of all that the selfish live for ? Humboldt wisely says that if every man is said to have his own des-tiny in his hands, that saying must be read to mean, not that he has the power to alter fate, but rather the power to make the best of bad fortune, and by his gentle acceptance of ill to transmute evil into good. Deprivations, small acts of self-abnegation which would have hurt another man, gave Dr. Faunthorpe a pleasant feeling, a genial sense of warmth and comfort in the region of the heart, which had the effect of whisky toddy or any other comfortable stimulant.

CHAPTER XI.

AT THE HOW.

SATURDAY shows bright and fair, a fine winter day, hoar frost on the hedges. The roads are dry, but not too hard for the horses; the minster towers stand out, sharply defined against the clear cold blue; rooks are screaming loud in the ragged elm boughs; robins singing merrily; a blithe day in the new born-year, a day which inspires Redcastle with the idea that trade is brisker than it has been, and things in general looking up, so potent is the influence of fine weather.

Never has Marion Faunthorpe felt so proud or happy as when her uncle's carriage calls for her and her boxes, and she takes her seat opposite Mr. Trenchard, who, by right divine of his three-score years and ten, occupies the post of honour wrapped to the chin in sable, and with a tiger-skin rug over his knees.

'Did you shoot that tiger yourself, dear uncle?' asks Marion, bent on making herself agreeable.

'No, child,' replies the dear uncle rather snappishly, 'I had something better to do in India than to shoot tigers.'

'But it's very nice shooting big game, isn't it, uncle? Some people go to India on purpose for that, don't they?'

'Fools do, perhaps. There's no accounting for their taste.'

The little surgeon has come out to the gate to see his niece off. Nay, he has actually stolen an hour from the parish in order to behold the glory of her departure. He seems as pleased to see her happiness as if he himself were going to the How, and at the last moment the girl feels touched.

'You dear, darling old uncle,' she says, hanging round his neck, and forgetting the possibility of damage to her new hat, 'how good you always are!—always—always—always, and I'm an ungrateful wretch.'

'My love, you are not ungrateful, and you have very little to be grateful for.'

'Everything you mean, uncle Robert. I shall think of you ever so many times a day at the How; and if the dinners are very nice I shall so wish you could be with us.'

'Thank you, my dear. I shall think of you, and miss you very much.'

'I'm going to keep house,' exclaims Jenny, lolling against the gate, and swaying to and fro distractingly as she talks; 'and make tea and all; nobody to tell me not to take too much butter; and Hester will give us my favourite puddings, I know, if I quill her cap borders.'

So after embracing the doctor in this demonstrative fashion, Marion enters the carriage with tears in her eyes, to the aggravation of Stephen Trenchard, who hates tears and fuss and emotion of all kinds, except the thrill of delight which accompanies a successful stroke of business.

'Crying again,' he exclaims testily. 'What's the matter now?'

'There's nothing the matter, dear uncle. Only I'm so happy; and I felt a little overcome at leaving uncle Robert.'

'It's a pity you should leave him at all if the parting is so pathetic,' sneers Mr. Trenchard.

'Oh, Sibyl, I've had such a nice little note from Miss Cardonnel to confirm Sir Wilford's invitation,' says Marion; and she exhibits a formal note, in which the polite Phœbe expresses her satisfaction at having heard from her brother that Miss Marion Faunthorpe has promised to accompany her sister on Saturday.

The drive is delightful for any one with an unburdened mind, and even Sibyl feels the sweetness of the clear winter air, and determines to make the best of an awkward concatenation of events. After all, it is better to be lolling in uncle Trenchard's carriage on one's way to a delightful old country house than to be grinding at French or German verbs in Mrs. Hazleton's cheerless second-floor schoolroom, badly warmed by a fire that seems always made of the dullest coals that ever came from the bosom of the earth. And all this is but the filling up of a gap in her life. This chasm of time bridged over and she will be with Alexis once more, and they will have uncle

Trenchard's money to spend and be happy ever afterwards. She has persuaded herself that let Alexis make what protestations he pleases in the present, he will take her to his heart again gladly when the fitting time comes.

'And in the meantime there is no use in my moping and making myself miserable,' reflects Sibyl, her spirits elevated by atmospheric in-fluences, and the prospect of being the object of general admiration.

'I wonder if there will be many people there?' she speculates presently.

'People with titles,' suggests Marion; 'a duke perhaps. I should like to see a duke—or a duchess. That would be better still. Think of her dresses, Sib. Must'nt they be magnificent!'

Sibyl smiles the languid smile of contempt at her sister's simplicity.

'As if there were a sliding scale for the toilet,' she says. 'Why, cotton spinners' wives dress as well as duchesses now-a-days. They employ the same milliners, and pay their bills quicker.'

'It's dreadful to think of,' replies Marion. 'It seems like turning things topsy-turvy, you know.'

They are at the How by this time, a domain which Marion enters open-eyed and dumb with awe. Sir Wilford comes out into the porch to receive them, and gives directions about their luggage, and makes himself generally busy. Then he calls out Phœbe and introduces Marion to her, at which Marion, being almost tongue-tied by shyness, says, 'Thank you.'

'You show the Miss Faunthorpes their rooms, Phœbe,' says the hospitable baronet; but this is a length to which Miss Cardonnel will not go, though she conducted her dearest Cecilia to her apartment half an hour ago with her arm round Cecilia's severely trained waist.

'Perker knows all about the rooms,' she says, whereupon appears the essence of respectability in a black silk gown and smart cap, otherwise Mrs. Perker the housekeeper.

Sibyl and Marion follow this personage up the broad oak staircase to a long perspective of corridor, in which Mrs. Perker opens two doors next each other, and reveals twin bedchambers neatly furnished with maple and chintz.

'I thought you two ladies would like to be next each other,' remarks the housekeeper obligingly, as if the choice of the rooms were entirely her own.

'We do, very much,' exclaims Marion, who regains her power of speech in this inferior presence. 'I'm very glad I'm to be near Sibyl. I should be awfully afraid of ghosts in this great rambling house.'

Mrs. Perker smiles condescendingly, as if she were a superior order of being, accustomed to large houses and family spectres.

'It is a rambling old place,' she says, 'but I shouldn't fancy myself in one of your fine lightsome modern houses, all glare and gilding.'

'And there is a ghost, I dare say,' says Marion, with thrilling interest.

The housekeeper screws up her lips and smiles significantly, as if she could, and if she would, tell of as many apparitions as appear in the tragedy of 'Macbeth.'

'There has never been a ghost owned to at the

How,' she says, 'and I wouldn't breathe the name of such a thing in Miss Cardonnel's hearing, but people *have* been frightened—strangers. It may have been rats, or it may have been the wind. I can't say. But there are friends of the family who wouldn't sleep in this corridor, no, not for a thousand pounds.'

Marion shudders, and almost wishes herself back in the shabby old house at the end of Redcastle.

'So here are your rooms, young ladies, opening into each other.'

'How nice!' exclaims Marion.

Never in her life has she felt more warmly attached to Sibyl than she does at this moment.

Fires burn cheerily in both rooms, and each apartment has that thoroughly comfortable and convenient air only to be seen in a well-ordered country house, and altogether distinct from the cheerless precision of an hotel bedchamber.

There is the nice little writing-table, with all things needful for correspondence, in front of the fire; the easy chair; the candles, and pincushion, and a hothouse flower or two in a slender glass on the dressing-table. All smiles a welcome to the stranger—not Miss Cardonnel's welcome, by the way, but Mrs. Perker's.

'I've given your maid a nice room on the second floor, within easy reach of this, ma'am,' says the housekeeper, at which Marion's eyes open wide with wonder.

'I have no maid,' replies Sibyl, unabashed by that humiliating fact ; 'I am accustomed to wait upon myself.'

'Indeed, ma'am. Some young ladies prefer it, I know. For my own part I couldn't bear anybody fidgeting about me. And if you should require any assistance Miss Cardonnel's maid will be very happy.'

'Thanks, no, my sister can help me if I want her.'

And Sibyl proceeds to open her handsome portmanteaus, while Marion contrives to stand before the shabby receptacle which contains her property, lest the scrutinizing eye of Mrs. Perker should behold its dilapidation.

The housekeeper bustles off, and leaves the two girls to themselves.

'It's rather like going to school again, isn't it, Sibyl?' inquires Marion, whose spirits have sunk a little, oppressed by the unfamiliar splendours of the How. 'I feel just as I did the day we went to Miss Worries, and I can't help fancying we shall be told off into our different classes when we go downstairs.'

'The sound of the luncheon-bell reminds the sisters that they have no time to waste, and they go downstairs together presently, conscious that they are looking nice enough to face even unfriendly criticism. Sir Wilford is lounging in the hall, and they go in to luncheon under his wing. Fred Stormont is near the dining-room door, and rushes to meet Sibyl and her sister; and Mrs. Stormont gives a friendly bow from the other end of the table, where she sits among the stately matrons and the bald-headed fathers of the land; and they begin to feel themselves more at home, as Marion whispers to her sister.

The conversation at luncheon runs more continuously upon the present company's absent brothers and sisters, and cousins, and nieces, and sons and daughters-in-law, than is quite congenial to the feelings of a stranger totally unacquainted with these relations, but Marion manages to get up a little talk about nothing particular with Fred Stormont, which, beheld from afar, looks like flirtation, and causes the young man's anxious mother to put up her gold eye-glass and look at him through it, wondering how that silly Frederick can be so ridiculous as to waste his attentions upon the wrong sister.

'I suppose Mr. Trenchard will leave the girl five thousand pounds or so,' thinks Mrs. Stormont, ' but what would be the use of that to a young man with Fred's expensive habits ? '

CHAPTER XII.

TILBERRY STEEPLECHASE.

THE guests assembled at the How soon divide them-
selves into sections or groups, like the various members of the lower animal creation. Mr. and Mrs.
Chasubel draw around them the more seriously
minded of the younger visitors,—Lavinia Cardonnel ;
Cecilia Hawtree, who has a poetical mind, and is
Anglican to the verge of Romanism ; Laura and
Mary Radnor, who are great upon church decoration
and choir singing; and some others. General
Mactower attracts the young men, as it were, into a
focus of sporting talk, varied with anecdotes of the
London world, which, according to the General, is
about as vile a world as could well exist without
calling down a burning fiery rain for its destruction.
Sir Wilford contrives to be attentive to all his guests,
but shows himself so particular in his devotion to
Sibyl that other people cannot afford to be uncivil

to her, even were they disposed to snub so **lovely a girl**.

The matrons **and** their daughters admit the fact of Miss Faunthorpe's beauty, but with certain **reservations.** They admire her complexion, **but** opine that its transparent purity **of** tint argues a consumptive tendency.

'And what a dreadful thing for poor Sir Wilford to marry a consumptive wife, my dear!' says Mrs. Radnor, in an awful voice.

'And to have consumptive children,' adds her daughter Laura.

'Poor little dears,' exclaims Miss Hawtree, compassionating the sorrows of these unborn infants in advance. 'I think it quite wicked of consumptive people to marry, don't you, Mrs. Radnor?'

'Yes, my love, there ought to be a law against **it.'**

'What pretty manners Miss Faunthorpe has!' remarks Mrs. Vernon, whose daughter possesses every attraction except good looks and agreeable manners,—'so sweet, so caressing. But don't you think—I hardly like to say it, for it sounds so

uncharitable, and I should be the last to say anything uncharitable after dear Mr. Chasubel's moving
discourse this morning,—don't you think she seems
rather artful ?'

'As deep as Garrick,' says the outspoken Mrs.
Radnor.

'She actually seems to discourage Sir Wilford's
attentions, quite pretends to avoid him, makes
believe to prefer ladies' society, when we all know
that she must be delighted at the idea of making
such a brilliant match.'

'When we know that the girl is brought here on
purpose to marry him,' rejoins Mrs. Radnor. 'The
old uncle has set his heart upon it, of course, and
will leave her the whole of his property, to the
detriment of her two sisters ; there's another girl at
Redcastle, Mrs. Stormont tells me. Very unjust, I
call it.'

This conversation takes place on Sunday afternoon, in a cosy circle round the morning-room fire,
while Sibyl and some of the younger guests are
walking in the park. Sunday evening affords an
opportunity for the display of musical genius, or

talent, as the case may be; and after the daughters
of the land have done the most **they** can with Miss
Lindsay's sacred ballads, Beethoven, Mozart,
Mendelssohn, and Chopin, Sibyl takes her turn
at the instrument, and surpasses **all her forerunners,**
not so much **by** the brilliancy of her **singing or**
playing **as by** the thought **and feeling which**
pervade both. In the long empty days at Lancaster
Lodge her piano has been her friend and companion,
the confidante of all **her** vague **regrets and fears,—**
her sorrowful love for her absent husband. Memory
and hope have spoken to her in many a tender strain
of Mozart's, in the deeper pathos of Beethoven, or
Mendelssohn's dreamy melody.

Sir Wilford Cardonnel knows very little about
music, save that of his hounds giving tongue in the
chill morning air that blows over heath and moor,
but he is not the less pleased **that Sibyl should excel**
in the musical **line.** His future wife ought to be an
accomplished person. He is glad, too, that she
should 'take **the shine'** out of Phœbe and Vinnie,
neither **of them** highly gifted by Apollo, though both
have laboured hard, and flourish **at a** quickish pace

through unmelodious fantasias, arpeggio-ing up and down the piano with a movement which their brother calls a rough gallop.

Altogether Sibyl is a success at the How. No one can dispute that. Marion looks on and wonders at her sister's calm acceptance of the general homage. She wears her honours as to the manner born, while Marion feels overpowered with shyness all through that aristocratic Sabbath; and says 'Thank you,' for everything, from an introduction or a compliment, to the too hasty removal of her plate by an all-accomplished serving-man.

By Monday morning, however, even Marion is quite at her ease, save for an inward awe of Phœbe and Lavinia who, behind their brother's back, give her a little of the *de haut en bas* manner by which intrusive commoners are crushed. But Fred Stormont takes her under his protection, and finding Sibyl unapproachable amidst her various admirers, consoles himself with a mild flirtation with Marion, to which even his watchful parent reconciles herself, reflecting that, after all, a dower of five thousand pounds—or possibly ten—is better than nothing, and that, no heiress being forthcoming, dear Frederick might make Marion happy by **proposing to her.**

After breakfast on Monday **there is a general** inspection **of the** stables, **at** which **even** Mr. Chasubel, the High Church parson, assists, **and in the** course **of which** he entertains the company **with** anecdotes of his hard riding days at Oxford, and **his** prowess in the hunting-field. The horses **are led out** for admiration, **and** the **guests commit** themselves to various opinions, at which the nether lips of the Yorkshire grooms work convulsively **in the** respectful endeavour to avoid a grin.

Tuesday **is the** race day, and there **is a consul-** tation as to how people are to go : the faster of the party—including all the young ladies—inclining **to** the saddle, **the middle-aged and** portly **being** satisfied with **a** seat **on** the drag, or **in** Miss **Cardonnel's barouche.**

'You **will** ride, of course ?' says **Sir** Wilford **to** Frederick.

'Oh, by all means; I shall **go** on the Dutchman. Here he is, poor old fellow, looking as fresh as paint,'

An officious boy has just led the bony gray into the quadrangle, where every eye is now directed to him.

'Why, where the deuce did you get that beast from, Cardonnel?' cries General Mactower, as the lad whisks off the Dutchman's checked raiment, and exhibits his angular haunches and dejected neck. 'Never saw such a screw in your stable.'

'It's Mr. Stormont's horse,' says the boy, grinning.

'Beg your pardon, Stormont,' says the General' 'I dare say he looks better in action. Very good for leather, no doubt.'

'He may not be much to look at,' says Fred, wounded yet apologetic, 'but he's a devil to go.'

'Ah. I dare say, those bony ones are sometimes.'

'Well, Stormont, you'll ride the Dutchman,' resumes Sir Wilford, 'that's capital. You can take care of Miss Marion Faunthorpe.'

'Delighted, I'm sure,' gasps Fred, with an inward sinking. He knows too well that on the Dutchman he has enough to do to take care of himself, and that a whole hunting-field might be spilt around him without his being able to afford help to the fallen.

'You haven't ridden much lately, I think you told me, Miss Marion,' says Sir Wilford to that young lady, who has been going into raptures about all the horses with long manes and sleek skins.

'Not since I was quite a little thing, but I idolize riding.'

'And you'll not be afraid to ride to Tilberry to-morrow. It's a nice quiet road.'

'I shall like it of all things.'

'Very well, Chanter, you must find me a safe mount for this young lady. She hasn't been riding much lately.'

'One of the old ones, eh, Sir Wilford?'

'Yes, old and steady. But something good to look at, you know.'

'There's Brown Fixture, Sir Wilford, an uncommon good 'oss, and as safe as a church.'

'Yes, Fixture 'll do, nothing like an old steeplechaser.'

'Fixture's as steady as a Christian,' says the groom, 'and such a memory too, nobody 'd think

how that 'oss do remember.   He ain't forgot the day
he bolted with Jem Kirk, tho' it's nigh seven year
ago.   He never do pass that corner o' th' 'eath but
what 'e'll prick up his old ears, and stick 'em
back'ards and give a bit of a quiver, as if he'd like
to have another lark.'

'He mustn't have any larks with Miss Faunthorpe,' says Sir Wilford.

'Lor, bless you, no, Sir Wilford, that's seven
year ago.   Fixture's as steady as a house.   The
smallest of our boys rides him beautiful.'

'Well, Miss Marion, I think you'll be safe on Fixture, especially with Stormont to take care of you.'

Marion looks gratefully at Frederick, with a
vague idea that he is going to escort her with a
leading rein, and that under his care she would be
safe upon the winner of the Leger.

'And now let's have a look at Juno,' says
Wilford.   'That's the mare I mean for you, Miss
Faunthorpe, and I think every one will allow she's
a perfect beauty.   My sister Phœbe wants her badly,
but I'm afraid of Phœbe's eleven stone.'

That substantially built damsel gives her brother

an indignant look at this brutal remark, which could
only come from one's own flesh and blood.

'When I want a horse I shan't ask you to choose
him for me, Wilford,' she says.

Juno is led forth and unveiled—a chestnut,
glossy as the nut itself when it bursts from its
green casing, and beautiful in form, with a small
head and a Greek profile—ox-eyed like her mighty
namesake.

'How lovely!' exclaim all the young ladies,
envying Sibyl.

This selection of the best horse in the stud for
Miss Faunthorpe is tantamount to a proposal, thinks
every one, and from this time forward Sibyl is regarded as the future Lady Cardonnel, and honoured
accordingly.

Has he or has he not proposed? the council of
matrons ask one another by-and-bye in the comfortable morning-room where they have assembled to
write their letters and read the newspapers.

The majority opine that the offer has been made
and accepted, and that Mr. Trenchard is here to
arrange about settlements.

'Phœbe Cardonnel must know,' hazards Mrs. Chasubel, this conversation taking place in the absence of the Miss Cardonnels, who are playing billiards with their younger guests.

'She may, but she's such a reserved girl, there's no getting anything out of her; and as it's evident that she and Lavinia hate the idea of their brother's marrying, it's a subject we can't approach very well.'

'I feel sure he has proposed,' says Mrs. Radnor. He looks as if it was a settled thing.'

'He may have settled it all in his own mind, but not yet declared himself,' responds Mrs. Chasubel. 'He must know that there is no chance of rejection.'

Mrs. Chasubel is right. Sir Wilford is fixed as fate, but has not yet found an opportunity to ask the fatal question. Sibyl is always in a crowd. She contrives to avoid anything approaching a *tête-à-tête*. And a man can hardly propose during a game of pyramids, or on a crowded drag with a spirited team in his hand, or as he hands his beloved a cup of tea at kettledrum time, or on the stairs, or in church.

Sir Wilford bides his time, therefore, and is patient.

The important Tuesday is a fine clear day, with a high wind, but no frost. Tilberry Races begin at half-past one, so there is no time for luncheon at the How, and a necessity for picnic baskets on the drag, very much to the delight of all the younger guests, who prefer to take their refreshment uncomfortably out of doors to the commonplace convenience of the dining-room.

At a quarter before one the horses and carriages are brought round to the porch, and Marion, in a borrowed habit and a chimney-pot hat, which is balanced rather hazardously on a small mountain of padded hair, awaits, with some faint apprehension, her first ride on anything larger than Tommy, the old pony.

She has not yet seen Brown Fixture, and as she stands on the top step with Fred Stormont at her side she surveys the animals timorously.

There is Juno, satin-skinned and proud of bearing, arching her graceful neck, and gazing pensively at the company with her ox-eyes, pawing the ground a little with one delicate hoof, as if eager to take flight. And here is Sibyl, looking her prettiest, a small, slender prettiness, in neatly fitting riding habit, and hat poised at exactly the right angle.

Sir Wilford is at hand to mount her, and there is the usual careful adjustment of stirrup and skirt, curb and snaffle.

'I wonder which is my horse?' says Marion, with an appealing look at Mr. Stormont.

'Which is Fixture, boy?' asks Fred of an attendant lad.

'This here, sir,' answers the youth.

'This here' is the animal in his charge, a tall brute, with a neck a yard long, and, in the language of the stable, too much daylight underneath.

'Good gracious!' cries Marion, appalled at the aspect of this animal, 'am I to go up there?'

'He's a big one, isn't he?' responds Fred. 'Capital stride I should think, get over plenty of ground in his gallop. Looks like an old steeplechaser, doesn't he?'

'He looks very dreadful,' says Marion dubiously.

'Oh, you needn't be afraid of him. He's steady enough, depend upon it. Sir Wilfred's head man wouldn't put you on an unsafe horse.'

'I hope not,' says Marion. 'But you'll take care of me, won't you, Mr. Stormont?'

'I'll do my best,' answers Fred. 'Ah, here's the Dutchman, rather fresh, I'm afraid.'

This last remark has reference to an uncouth attempt of the Dutchman to back into an adjacent shrubbery, on being dragged out of which he entangles himself clumsily with the other horses.

The drag and barouche have driven off by this time, and everybody is mounted except Marion and her swain.

Mounting Marion upon Fixture is not the easiest operation in mechanics. She gives a tremendous spring, but always at the wrong moment, and after two or three false starts she is hoisted to a level with Fixture's saddle, only to remain there suspended in mid air until allowed to slide gently to earth again.

'I'm afraid I'm not a good hand at mounting a lady,' murmurs the patient Frederick, after he has made himself almost apoplectic in the endeavour, and now an experienced groom comes forward, tells Marion exactly at what angle to put her left leg, and throws her up into the saddle as if she were a ball.

'Gracious!' she exclaims, 'I'm here at last, but oh, how high it is!'

She surveys the earth beneath her with a sense of awe; it is like being on a mountain top, and not half so safe. She gives a little cry of surprise when Fixture begins to move, as if motion were the last thing one might expect from a horse.

The rest of the riders have gone down the avenue, Sir Wilford riding Bull of Bashan, and keeping close beside Sibyl on Juno.

Frederick now clambers upon the Dutchman, who to the last moment struggles to elude his half-proprietor, as if desirous to prove that a horse cannot serve two masters. Fixture caracoles gently upon the gravel sweep while Fred is mounting, but even these gentle movements strike terror to the unaccustomed soul of Marion.

'I'm afraid he's very spirited,' she remarks to one of the grooms.

'Lord, mum, he's nigh twelve year old, there's none too much sperit in him. You'd best ride him on the curb if you're any ways timid.'

'Which is the curb?' inquires Marion.

The man shows her, and adjusts her reins, which she has been clutching in her right hand in au inextricable tangle.

'But do you think I can manage him with the reins in my left hand?' she asks. 'It seems so left-handed, I'm afraid I shan't have any power over him.'

'You can hold on with both hands if you're timersome, miss, but the lighter you handle Fixture the better. He's got a very nice mouth, and he don't stand being sawed at. Ride him on the curb if you like, but let your 'and foller 'is 'ed.'

This language is as dark as Hebrew to Marion. She has but one thought, and that is that she would fain be at rest in the barouche or the drag, nay, safe at home in the obscurity of domestic life, with cross Hester and impertinent Jane. Anywhere, any-where, off the back of Brown Fixture, who has just caught sight of some obnoxious object, and has made himself into an arch from which Marion feels as if she were sliding.

Fred has now brought the Dutchman so far into subjection as to turn his nose towards the avenue, and Fixture being clutched and jerked in the same direction by Marion, the two set out, as uncomfortable a couple as ever enjoyed the delights of equestrian exercise. When they are well out of ear-shot the grooms and boys burst into a simultaneous guffaw.

'After this we must have some beer,' says the head man. 'I'm blest if ever I see such a brace o' cockneys. I ain't had such a laugh since Chrizzlemas.'

Fixture proves himself worthy of his reputation, and goes down the avenue with amiable sobriety, nay, would be perfect in his conduct were it not for that brute the Dutchman, who shies at sight of a rabbit, wheels round altogether at sight of a rook, and otherwise disgraces himself by convulsive movements and collapses which disturb Fixture's equanimity, though he evidently regards them with contempt. The brown horse behaves so well, how-

ever, that when **they** have walked down the avenue
and emerged upon **the road**, Marion begins **to feel**
quite easy in her mind, **and to** think **that after all**
she really does doat upon riding.

But for the Dutchman's evil example **Fixture**
would behave admirably all the way to Tilberry, a
nice level road, with little to alarm a reasonable
equine mind. The Dutchman is, however, a creature
without reasonableness of mind, and contrives to
see objects of horror in the clearest road, whereby
Marion is every now and then startled from her
equanimity by a sudden bouncing of Mr. Stormont's
horse against hers, a movement by which she
narrowly escaped being pushed into a ditch.

'Isn't your **horse** a little wrong in **his mind,**
Mr. **Stormont?'** she asks, after one **of** these **en-**
counters. 'He puts his ears back in such **a** dreadful
way, and starts and plunges so awfully.'

'**Only high spirit,**' replies Fred, 'all thorough-
breds do it.'

'Then I think **I'd rather** ride an unthorough-
bred,' says Marion.

When they have **walked** for about **half a mile**

Frederick suggests a gentle trot, to which proposal Marion acquiesces smilingly. But the very beginning of the gentle trot makes her breathless, and she finds herself jerked about in her saddle in a most ferocious way. She holds on to the reins, however, with both hands, and endures stoutly, till Fred, in charity, reins in the Dutchman, whereupon Fixture stops as if some spring had been touched in his internal economy, and nearly pitches Marion out of the saddle by the suddenness of his stoppage.

'I'm afraid you don't quite enjoy trotting,' says Fred.

Marion pants for a little while, struggling with the innumerable hair-pins which sustain her pyramid of plaits, before she can recover breath enough to answer.

'I dare say it's very nice,' she replies at last, 'but it jerks one, don't you think? Perhaps Fixture is not a good trotter?'

'I think if you were to rise with him, and sit a little more in the middle of your saddle, you might find it more comfortable,' suggests Frederick.

'Do you think so? I'll try next time.'

Fred endeavours to explain the theory of trotting, which, although he has not quite conquered the practice, is firmly impressed upon his mind.

'Now,' he says, flattering himself that he has made it all clear, 'suppose we try again?'

A shake of the reins makes the Dutchman lunge violently forward as if he wanted to dash his brains out upon the road, and starts Fixture in a really delightful trot, if poor Marion only knew it. She bobs up and down as if she were bathing, but when she rises the horse doesn't, and the effect is even more jerky than before. She is just beginning to despair, when the red glow of a cottage fire, shining through an open door, appals the Dutchman's soul, and sends him into a wild canter, in which Fixture immediately joins. The horses tear along the road like the herd of swine driven down a steep place, and Marion, frightened, but rather enjoying the swinging pace, finds herself rising in her saddle as high as anyone could desire.

Inspired by the clatter of their hoofs the brutes rush on for some distance, Fred as powerless to pull up the Dutchman as he would be to stop a steam

engine at express pace, or stay the passage of the
north wind.   When the horses have had enough
they stop.

'I think I rose pretty well then,' remarks Marion,
self-complacently.

'Just now, when you were cantering ?'

'Yes.'

'But you oughtn't rise in the canter, you know,'
says Fred. 'You must sit as if you were part of
your horse; 'sit down on him and ride him,' as the
jockeys say.'

'Good gracious! It's very puzzling,' exclaims
Marion.

'All practice.   You must contrive to ride more.'

'Yes, I should like it above all things.   Uncle
Trenchard has bought Sibyl a horse.   But I am not
so favoured.'

'Ah, it's a good thing to be the favourite, isn't
it ?'

That canter has brought them nearly to the racecourse.   They overtake the rest of their party, Sibyl
looking as cool and comfortably upon Juno as if she
were sitting in her favourite easy chair at Lancaster

Lodge, while Marion is painfully conscious that the last half-hour's unaccustomed exercise has made an object of her.

'How have you enjoyed your ride?' asks Sibyl, coming to her side.

'Oh, pretty well,' replies Marion, rather crossly. 'I'm not accustomed to riding, like you, you know I haven't a horse of my own. Isn't my hair dreadful?'

'It's rather rough. But that doesn't matter.'

'Oh, not in the least—to you.'

'How do you like Fixture?' asks Sir Wilford, coming up to them.

'Very well, thank you. But I think he uses the wrong legs when he trots.'

Tilberry racecourse is a long strip of meadow land by the side of a river, rather a dreary scene on a gray winter's day, were it not for the carriages, horses, tax carts, and various vehicles which enliven it, and the eager crowd on foot.

Sir Wilford and his party are the most important group upon the ground, the rest of the assembly consisting chiefly of tenant farmers and their families, with a sprinkling of the Redcastle tradespeople, and a few smart carriages belonging to the manufacturing classes, chiefly noticeable for the newness of their harness, the splendour of their liveries, and the indifferent quality of their horses.

Sir Wilford pats Fixture's neck with a friendly air as he stands beside Marion.

'Poor old Fixture. Capital fellow he used to be six or seven years ago. I've ridden him many a time over this very course. Won a cup with him once, poor old chap. I wonder if he remembers?'

'Where's the steeple, Sir Wilford?' asks Marion, looking round at the landscape.

'The what?'

'The steeple. It's a steeplechase, isn't it?'

Sir Wilford smiles at the damsel's innocence.

'Steeplechase—across country, you know, and all that. There's no necessity for a steeple.'

'Oh, I thought you chose a steeple, and then rode straight to it, over hedges and ditches, and everything.'

'We've sunk the steeple. But we go over the hedges and ditches. There's the saddling bell. Yes, Fixture does remember.

'I wish he didn't,' says Marion nervously, as the animal pricks up his ears, and begins to curvet in a restless manner, which makes it rather difficult to hold him.

The equestrians are drawn up in a line by the side of the racecourse. There are no railings to divide the course from the rest of the meadow. It is only marked out by a line of sods turned up by the spade, and a post at intervals. The timber jumps are by no means desperate, and are well guarded by furze bushes; the water jump is a muddy ditch about twenty feet broad.

'I wish you'd hold him for me,' says Marion, appealing to Mr. Stormont. 'He's been so dreadfully excited since that bell rang.'

Fred clutches at Fixture's rein for a minute or so, and tries at the same time to soothe the Dutchman, who has just expressed his antipathy to a very small child in a pinafore, eating a large piece of parliament.

Fixture shuffles about a little, and then seems to grow calm. Sir Wilford and his party ride up and down, impatient for the beginning of the sport.

Marion and her protector keep together by the course.

The bell rings again, louder this time. There is a gust of excitement in the very wind. The signal is given, the gaily coloured jackets blaze out against the cold gray sky, the horses are off with a rush—. Fixture following them.

He has stood like a statue to see them go by, then, as they passed him, he has gathered himself together, and pursued them like a maniac. The old steeplechaser has not forgotten his trade.

There is a cry of horror from Sir Wilford and his party, a roar—half terror, half laughter—from the crowd, as Marion is borne along, her arms frantically encircling the animal's neck, her plaits flying in the wind, her shrill shrieks ringing out upon the air. She drops something at every stage of her journey. First her whip, then her handkerchief, then her hat, then one of the plaits, an artificial enrichment which she has deemed a necessary appendage to a very good head of hair. On flies Fixture, struggling for a place, feeling that he must win or perish in the attempt. Marion, with her face buried in his mane, sees nothing, knows nothing, except that she is miraculously holding on somehow, and that sudden death is imminent. The timber jump is before them, and the spectators hold their breaths, anticipating a fearful fall, perhaps a deadly one, when Sir Wilford gallops across on Bull of Bashan, and contrives to catch Fixture's bridle just as he his lifting himself to the leap.

The old steeplechaser swings on one side and lands Marion comfortably on the turf, where she lies motionless till kindly hands raise her. She is only stunned, and comes to her senses after a minute or so to find herself the centre of a sympathetic crowd.

'Poor dear!' says a woman, 'she did hold on well, didn't she? It was beautiful.'

Sibyl is on the scene by this time, and dismounts to assist the fallen one.

'You're not hurt, are you, dear?' she inquires, anxiously.

'I don't know whereabouts it is,' replies Marion, clutching her dishevelled plaits, 'but I feel as if I was all but killed—somewhere.'

Brandy flasks are produced, and the sufferer is

persuaded to take two or three sips of the spirit.

'Back all right, I hope,' says Sir Wilford, who has delivered over the excited Fixture to a groom.

'I feel as limp as if it was broken,' replies Marion. 'When did I fall? was it the day before yesterday, or longer ago than that?'

'My love, it was just this minute.'

'Then I've had a long dream,' replies Marion, putting her hand to her head; 'such a long dream. I feel as if I had been riding steeplechases on horrid runaway horses for the last three weeks.'

'I shall never forgive myself for putting you on Fixture,' says Sir Wilford, with a conscience-stricken air, 'but I really thought he was the quietest old horse in the stable.'

'Oh, I don't mind it a bit,' answers Marion, who enjoys being the object of general attention. 'In fact, I rather like it. It's very exciting, you know.'

'Uncommonly,' mutters Sir Wilford, who has had as bad a fright as he ever experienced in his life. 'I thought you were done for when he came to that fence. If it hadn't been for the Bull—well, we won't talk about it.'

Here a small boy brings Marion the fallen plait of false hair, which looks something like a defunct snake as he hands it to her, whereat there is a faint titter.

After twisting herself about a little in the arms of her supporters, Marion announces that she has no bones broken, to her knowledge.

'My spine may go all wrong to-morrow, and make me a cripple for life,' she says, 'but I think I can walk now.'

'Shall I mount you again, ma'am?' asks the groom, who is holding Fixture. That quadruped is bathed in perspiration, stands like a block of wood, and droops his head despondently as if fully aware that he has made a fool of himself. 'You might ride him home safe enough, ma'am. He's quiet now.'

'What, get upon *him* again?' cries Marion. 'No, thank you.'

'Bring her to the barouche,' says Sir Wilford, and Marion is led to that vehicle, where the Miss

Cardonnels inform her that they have been suffer-
ing agonies of anxiety on her behoof, though neither
they nor Mrs. and Miss Radnor have left their
seats.

'We knew we could be no use,' Phœbe remarks,
apologetically, 'and we should have only increased
the confusion if we had come to you.'

'It's such a dangerous thing to ride when one
is not used to it,' remarks Vinnie, soothingly.
'Wilford ought to have known better than to put
you on that dreadful old horse.'

Marion, who felt herself a person of importance
amidst the crowd on the race course, shrinks into
dire insignificance amongst these fine ladies in the
carriage. She is screwed in, bodkin, between Phœbe
and Mrs. Radnor. She knows she is looking an
object in her battered hat and disordered tresses,
and she can see nothing whatever of the race. The
four ladies talk their usual family talk of uncles
and cousins, nephews and nieces, and people they
know; discuss the domestic affairs of the niece who
is just married; review the prospects of the nephew
who is going to marry; talk about the cousin who

has just had a baby, and the unjust will of the uncle lately deceased; until Marion absolutely wishes herself away from these privileged ones, and thinks how nice it would be to be reading a novel on the parlour sofa at uncle Robert's, the sofa wheeled cosily up to the fire, and Jenny kneeling on the hearth toasting muffins.

'If my back *is* broken, it'll be a comfort to be a doctor's niece,' she tells herself consolingly.

It is dusk when the last race is run, and the How party turn their faces homeward. A three-mile ride in the winter twilight lies between them and kettledrum; an excellent opportunity for a *tête-à-tête* with Sibyl, thinks Sir Wilford, who has found it impossible to secure half an hour of that young lady's society at the How. There she is always surrounded.

He contrives to leave the course close at her side, and to keep well in front of the other equestrians. Bull is quiet enough now, and quite content to lapse into a lazy walk, having been indulged with half a dozen tearing gallops across the level ground near the race-course. Juno and Bull step side by side, solemnly as a pair of Flemish funeral horses, which have never done anything but 'black work' since they were foaled.

It is a fine level road, a copse on one side, the moor upon the other. Wintry stars begin to twinkle in the gray, cottage fires gleam now and then across the road.

'Now is my time,' thinks Sir Wilford.

'I hope you are not frightened at riding in the dark,' he begins, with a gush of originality.

'Not at all. In the first place I don't call this gray twilight darkness, and in the second place I feel myself quite safe in your care.'

'I am glad of that,' says Sir Wilford. 'I am very glad you feel yourself safe with me, Sibyl.'

This is the casting of the die. After this utterance of her Christian name Sir Wilford feels he has committed himself to the deed. Receding now were as difficult as to go on.

'Yes, Sibyl, I am glad, for I want to be your protector all the days of my life. I want this dear little hand,' taking the hand that droops carelessly at her side, with gold-handled whip lightly held,

'I want this hand for mine. Oh, I think you must have seen ever so long ago that I love you. I have made no secret of my attachment, Sibyl. You are the **first** woman I ever met that I would care to make mistress of the **How—you are the** only woman I ever have asked—the only woman I ever shall ask to be my wife.'

'Oh, stop, stop, **Sir** Wilford! Not one **word** more!' cries Sibyl. 'Forgive me for having let you say so much.'

While he has been talking she has decided on her course. A bold step, but the only one open to her. This young man **is** honourable, generous-minded. She will, she must trust him with her secret.

'Forgive you, Sibyl, for what?'

'Forgive me, if you ever can. I have been **so** wrong. I have acted **so** meanly. **Forgive** me for **not** having understood **you better, for** not having told you the truth about myself. I have led you **on** perhaps, **most unwillingly,** but **still I** may have led you **on to** make this **generous** offer.'

'Generous **be** hanged!' cries the impetuous **Sir**

Wilford. 'There's no generosity in a man trying to get the thing he most desires. Don't talk about leading me on, Sibyl. Of course, you led me on— that is to say, you couldn't help seeing that I love you to distraction, and you've let me go on loving you. There's no leading a fellow on in that. You're like one of the stars up yonder, and just let yourself be admired. But you're not going to reject me, Sibyl. I can't believe that.'

He does not believe it. Upon his own personal merits he has formed no decided opinion. He knows that he is tolerably good-looking, does justice to his tailor's handiwork, rides straight to hounds, and is free from vice. But he puts himself out of the scale altogether, and reckons upon his position and surroundings. That there is any woman in Yorkshire who would refuse to be mistress of the How and the How stables is more than he can believe.

'You won't reject me, Sibyl?' he repeats.

'Indeed, Sir Wilford, I have no alternative. I can make you but one answer.'

'And that is——'

' No.'

' Oh, come, you can't mean it, Sibyl.'

' I do mean it.'

' You're in love with some other fellow. Not that cur, Fred Stormont, I hope ? '

' If I thought about Mr. Stormont at all I should detest him.'

' Who is it, then ? '

' Sir Wilford, will you keep a secret if I confide one to you ? '

' Have I any claim to be considered a gentle-man ? '

' Yes, yes, I know I may trust you.'

' Go on,' says Sir Wilford, sunk in gloom.

' You know very little of my history, I think, Sir Wilford,' begins Sibyl, in a low but steady voice, ' although you have done me the greatest honour in your power to confer upon me. Perhaps all you know is that I have been adopted by my uncle Stephen, and that he is likely to leave me a fortune. I have no certainty that he will do so, but I have every reason to believe it.'

' Yes, yes. I know all about that.'

'But you do not know, perhaps, that when my uncle came from India I was absent from Red-castle. I had gone to London to get my living as a governess. It was a dreary life, and would have seemed drearier, I dare say, but for one event which happened to diversify it. I was weak enough to fall in love with a gentleman who had as little to marry upon as I had.'

'Poor child! Passing fancy—romantic attachment. You'll outlive that, Sibyl.'

'It will outlive me, for we contrived to make the bond lasting. Without the knowledge of any of my family I was foolish enough to get married! The man I married is the son of Mr. Trenchard's worst enemy. My only chance of inheriting my uncle's fortune was the concealment of my marriage. I have therefore contrived to keep the secret, and you are the first to whom I have ever revealed it. If you betray me I am ruined.'

'Betray you! What do you take me for?' cries Sir Wilford. 'You are a married woman, and your husband is living?'

'Yes.'

'And he suffers you to keep up this deception
—to stoop to this meanness. Forgive me——'

'For calling things by their right names—yes,
I forgive you. There are no words too hard for my
conduct; and yet, perhaps, if you could measure the
depth of misery I had sunk into before I made up
my mind to try for uncle Trenchard's fortune, even
you might pity me.'

'Pity! Yes, Sibyl, I pity you with all my heart;
but I can't help despising your husband.'

'Do not despise him. What I have done has
been done without his knowledge or consent. He
only traced me to my present home a very little
while ago, and he then told me that he would
repudiate me and my fortune when the day came
for me to possess it.'

'And yet you continue the deception?'

'Would it not be positive idiocy to abandon it
just now, when the end is in all probability very
near? My uncle has not many years to live.'

'He looks rather shaky, poor old fellow—liver, I
dare say.'

'Why should I make a revelation that would be

a shock to him, and do no good to any one else? If my husband really loves me he will be true to me as I am to him, and all will be well for us by-and-bye.'

'And you'll secure the old man's money,' says Sir Wilford. 'Trust a woman for looking after the main chance.'

'You despise me, Sir Wilford,' falters Sibyl humiliated.

'No, no; nothing of the kind. Only when one comes to talk of money it takes a little of the bloom off, you know. I had looked up to you as an angel—something quite ethereal, you know. And when one comes down to pounds, shillings, and pence—well, it's rather a long way to come, you know.'

'You'll keep my secret?'

'Consider it buried in the deepest grave that ever was dug.'

'And if you are tempted to despise, if you do despise me, as I fear you must, try to remember that you have never known what it is to be poor, that there is a depth of misery; abject fear for to-morrow's bread; the dread of being turned out of one's wretched shelter into the street, the horror of being clothed in rags, driven to the workhouse. Consider that you have never known these things. I have, and my deception grew out of them. If I told the truth to-morrow I might have to go back to all those unforgotten horrors. If I play my part steadily to the end, I may secure a happy future for my husband and myself.'

'Upon my word it's a very trying position, Miss Faunthorpe, and I feel for you with all my heart. It would have been kinder to me if you had given me a hint of the truth a little sooner, and spared me—well, spared me a very bitter disappointment. Yet I can but thank you for having trusted me at the last.'

'One word more, Sir Wilford. Pray do not let my uncle suppose that you have asked me to be your wife. He would never forgive me for my rejection of you.'

'I'll take care of that. He shall think me the most miserable object in creation—a male flirt—a man who dangles about a pretty woman meaning nothing but his own amusement. I'll bear the brunt of the old gentleman's anger, Miss Faunthorpe, rely upon it; and if ever you want a friend, remember that, in spite of his disappointment, Wilford Cardonnel is yours to the death!'

CHAPTER XIII.

JOEL PILGRIM.

THAT evening after Tilberry races is the gayest night there has yet been at the How. There is a dinner party, matrons and maidens wear their finest dresses, each assuming that one last and newest fashion which the Princess Metternich, or some one of equal importance, has made the rage in Paris. Even poor Marion, revived by strong tea and an hour's comfortable slumber, puts on her blue and salmon dinner dress, and feels that she is looking lovely.

Yet, although most of the ladies at the How are tolerably satisfied with their own appearance, there is none among them who would venture to deny Sibyl Faunthorpe's claim to that apple of discord from whose pips sprang Troja's fall, and the slaughter of many heroes. She is paler than usual this evening, but her eyes are bright with a feverous excitement, and there is more brilliancy in her pallor than in other women's carnation.

Mr. Trenchard observes that look of unusual excitement, and sees that the hand which waves the large white fan trembles a little now and then. He has heard from some friendly gossips how Sir Wilford and Sibyl rode on ahead of all the others during the return home, and he draws his own conclusions from Sibyl's suppressed agitation and this fact. The baronet has proposed, he tells himself, Sibyl is to all intents and purposes mistress of fortune and the How. Mr. Trenchard rejoices in this consummation as if it took a load off his mind. He smiles sweetly upon his niece, and once, when he is near her for a few minutes before they go to dinner, he ventures to hint at his thoughts.

'How pretty you are looking, my pet!' he whispers, 'but a little over-excited. You have something to tell me, haven't you?'

'Nothing out of the common, dear uncle.'

'What, not about your ride home? Come, you see a little bird has been before you.'

'Little birds are generally more inventive than veracious, uncle.'

And at this point the bachelor appointed to that honour offers Sibyl his arm, and the procession files off to the dining-room. The long drawing-room, once a chapel, is at its fullest about an hour after dinner. Sibyl has just risen from the piano, where she has played Chopin and Schumann to the delight, real or affected, of her auditory. Stephen Trenchard stands with his back to the low marble chimney-piece, surveying the room in which his lovely niece forms so important a feature, flattering himself with the fancy that this room will be hers before long, that she will be its acknowledged mistress as she is now its queen.

He looks round for Sir Wilford, wondering not to see that captive of love exhibiting his fetters more conspicuously, but Sir Wilford is standing on the hearth-rug at the other end of the room—there are two fireplaces in the drawing-room—talking hunting talk with a brace of rubicund sportsmen who look as if their systems were permeated with old port.

While Mr. Trenchard is wondering that Sir

Wilford should hold himself thus aloof from the object of his devotion, the butler throws open a distant door, and announces—

'Mr. Joel Pilgrim.'

Everybody looks up at the announcement, and at the entrance of the person to whom the name belongs. The name is strange to all ears save Mr. Trenchard's. The person is a stranger to all eyes save Mr. Trenchard's and Sibyl's.

Not a welcome announcement, by any means, judging by the sudden angry look that darkens Stephen Trenchard's countenance, spreading over it an additional shade of sallowness, deepening the bistre beneath his eyes, hardening the lines about his mouth.

He crosses the room hurriedly, and takes the stranger by the hand. 'My dear Pilgrim, what brings you here? At so late an hour, too.'

'I have to apologize for what must naturally appear an intrusion,' replies Mr. Pilgrim, in a voice which is peculiarly soft and conciliatory, 'but the commercial man's habitual selfishness is my only excuse—if a vice can be an excuse for a solecism.

I wanted to see you to ask your advice upon an affair of considerable moment. I went to Redcastle, found you were staying here, and hired a fly to bring me on. The roads were dark, the horse slow, and the flyman stupid. Thus I am above an hour later than I need have been, though in any case I must have been late, as I only reached Redcastle at seven o'clock.'

'You might have waited till to-morrow,' says Mr. Trenchard, unappeased by this apology.

'I was too anxious to wait. I hope Sir Wilford Cardonnel and his family will pardon my impertinence.'

He looks towards Sir Wilford, who has come forward at the announcement of a guest.

'Very happy to see any friend of Mr. Trenchard's,' says the good-natured baronet. 'I'm afraid you have had a cold drive.'

'It is not particularly warm upon your moors for a man born in Calcutta.'

'Have you dined, by the way?'

'I dined by the way. I stopped in Redcastle just long enough to dine.'

'You mustn't go back to-night,' says Sir Wilford, hospitably. 'You can have your chat with your friend Mr. Trenchard in the library, and then come back to us to finish the evening. I'll order a room to be got ready for you.'

'You are really too good,' replies Mr. Pilgrim, hesitating, and with a glance at Mr. Trenchard.

'But you have no valise,' interjects Stephen Trenchard, 'impossible for you to stay. Come to the library, and I'll soon settle this business for you.'

Mr. Pilgrim smiles a subdued smile, murmurs his grateful acknowledgment of Sir Wilford's kindness, and bows himself out after Stephen Trenchard. There is a general sense of relief among the company when that sleek head and swarthy face are withdrawn from their midst.

'What a peculiar-looking person!' exclaims Mrs. Stormont, who is sitting near Sibyl.

'What an unpleasant-looking person!' responds the outspoken Mrs. Radnor.'

'Do you know him, Sibyl?' inquires Mrs. Stormont.

'I have seen him—once before. He is an Indian friend of my uncle's.'

'He has never stayed at Lancaster Lodge, I think,' hazards Mrs. Stormont.

'No, he has never stayed there. He only called one evening on business.'

'He must live in the neighbourhood then, I suppose?'

'I should hardly think so.'

Curiosity has been awakened by this late visitor. There is something out of the common in his appearance, and Mr. Trenchard's vexation at his coming has been tolerably apparent to every one.

Mr. Trenchard and his friend are closeted in the library for about an hour, then a bell rings, and the stranger is conducted back to his fly, whose departing wheels are heard in the drawing-room half an hour after all other guests have gone, and just as the house party are bidding one another good night. It is a quarter past twelve.

'I wonder Mr. Trenchard has not let that poor man stay,' says Mrs. Stormont; 'a nasty drive back to Redcastle at this time of night—such a horrid road after dark,—and those flymen are tipsy half their time.'

'Perhaps Mr. Trenchard wouldn't much care if the man were turned over into a ditch,' rejoins Mrs. Radnor. 'He's the most unpleasant-looking person I ever saw. Did you see how those black eyes of his seemed to take us all in? He's just my idea of a Thug.'

Mrs. Stormont has no very clear notion of Thugs, but admits that the stranger's expression has impressed her unfavourably.

At breakfast the next morning there is general surprise when Mr. Trenchard announces his intention of returning to Redcastle in the course of the day. He has had letters from India which demand his attention—he has some property over there which the Government talk of buying,—and it will be very advantageous for him if the transaction comes off. It is a matter which requires prompt negotiation.

'I am extremely sorry to curtail such a pleasant visit, especially on account of these girls,' he adds.

The Misses Cardonnel express their deep regret,
but do not urge Mr. Trenchard to reconsider his
decision. Sir Wilford expresses his sorrow, but
even he does not press his guests to remain, much to
the surprise of the lookers on, who speculate curiously on Mr. Trenchard's motive for going, and Sir
Wilford's reason for taking his sweetheart's departure
so easily.

'Don't you see that it's all settled between
them?' says Mrs. Radnor to Mrs. Chasubel. 'He
has made her an offer and been accepted, and I dare
say the old man wants to consult his lawyers about
settlements. He'll give her a fortune on her marriage,
no doubt.'

Sibyl is very glad to go, though she feels much
more comfortable in Sir Wilford's society now that
he and she understand each other. Marion is bitterly disappointed at this abrupt termination to her
visit, and is inclined to grumble about the money
wasted on those lovely dresses, till she reflects that
the money was not hers, and that it is something
to have secured the dresses. There will be some
pleasure in disporting herself before Maria Harrison

in that brown silk costume. So the sisters go
upstairs and pack, aided, or in some measure hin-
dered, by Miss Cardonnel's maid, whose services that
young lady politely offers for the occasion. Mrs.
Parker is rewarded for her civilities, morning cups
of tea and other small attentions, and before luncheon
all is ready for departure. Mr. Trenchard has sent
a groom to Redcastle to order his carriage to fetch
him at three o'clock. Sir Wilford is absent from
the luncheon table for the first time since the
coming of his guests. Phœbe and Lavinia are un-
usually cheerful ; indeed, Sibyl fancies that there is a
general accession of cheerfulness among the feminine
portion of the community. The gentlemen, on the
other hand, deplore Miss Faunthorpe's departure
with a flattering vehemence. They declare that a
star is about to vanish from their sky, and a good
deal more to the same effect. Even Mr. Chasubel
has admired Sibyl, and has told people in confidence
that she is the image of a Madonna by Guido in the
Vatican, a nice way of telling people that he has
been in Rome, and is an art critic in his way. Fred
Stormont sits next to Marion and bewails his loss.

'We ought to have gone out riding together ever so many times more,' he says. 'I should have made you a first-rate horsewoman,' an assertion that savours of rashness when it is remembered that Mr. Stormont has not yet succeeded in making himself a capable horseman.

At three o'clock Mr. Trenchard's carriage is at the door, the portmanteaus are in, the servants feed, and all things ready. Just at this last moment Sir Wilford appears, looking very much like his own gamekeeper, in velveteen coat, cords, and leather gaiters, and with his gun in his hand.

'I hope you'll all excuse me for forgetting the luncheon-bell,' he says to the company generally, most of whom have come out into the hall to say good-bye to Mr. Trenchard and his nieces. 'The birds were very wild, and Glenny and I forgot the progress of the enemy. I made quite a rush home to say good-bye to Mr. Trenchard.'

'It will not be a long parting, I hope,' replies Stephen Trenchard. 'You must come and dine with us directly you are free.'

'I shall be charmed. Good-bye, Miss Faunthorpe.'

Sibyl and Sir Wilford shake hands, at least thirty pair of eyes watching the operation. They shake hands in a formal and orthodox manner, and no one can detect so much as a secret pressure—love's Masonic grip. He leads her to the carriage, and when she is seated, and the coachman has gathered up the reins, he leans over for the last word, and one last pressure of the little hand he had hoped to make his own.

'Trust me,' he says. 'You have almost broken my heart, but you may trust me.'

Mr. Trenchard is silent and gloomy throughout the homeward drive. Sibyl, although glad to be separated from Sir Wilford, looks forward despondently to the solitude and monotony of her life at Lancaster Lodge after the gaiety and variety of the last few days. At the How she has not had leisure for sad thoughts! no time for self-reproach, regret, and all the illness that attends her selfish course. She has been the centre of an admiring circle, her vanity gratified to the uttermost, and life has seemed one round of pleasure.

Marion is loquacious as usual, and rattles on

with her criticisms upon The How and its visitors, from Mrs. Radnor's exaggerated aquiline nose, which always blushed after luncheon, 'as if it was ashamed of belonging to any one who drank so much sherry,' says Marion, to the Miss Vernons' high-heeled boots, ' in which I know they suffer agonies,' adds Marion.

Neither Stephen Trenchard nor Sibyl responds to these remarks, but the babble runs on intermittingly till they come to the lower end of the town, and to uncle Robert's green garden gate.

Jenny, the omnipresent, rushes out at the sound of the carriage wheels, her hair flying in the wind, and receives her sister with a volley of 'goodness graciouses,' and ' sure to goodnesses,' and numerous embraces which are like the gambadoes of an infant hippopotamus, or the friskings of a friendly sea-lion.

Mr. Trenchard gives a sigh of relief when Marion and her boxes have been deposited; nor is Sibyl sorry to dispense with her sister's viva-cious society.

' You will find a visitor at my house, Sibyl,' says

Stephen Trenchard, as they drive towards the Bar, 'a visitor whom I expect you to treat with all consideration, as he is a particular friend of mine.'

'Mr. Pilgrim, uncle?' asks Sibyl, startled.

'Yes, Mr. Pilgrim. I did not wish him to take advantage of Sir Wilford's hospitality, nor did I want him to go back to London without proper entertainment, so I invited him to spend a week or so at Lancaster Lodge.'

'And that was the reason you left the How so soon?'

'That and other reasons influenced me. There is that property I spoke about at luncheon.'

'To be sure; I forgot that.'

'I hope my leaving so suddenly has not been a disappointment to you, Sibyl?'

'Not at all, dear uncle.'

'And that I have in no way prevented the triumph which I fully expected you to win. Pray be candid with me, my dear child. Sir Wilford has proposed to you, and you have accepted him? You ought to have hastened to tell me of an event which you know must give me unalloyed pleasure.'

'My dear uncle, I have nothing to tell. I am as far from being Lady Cardonnel as ever I was in my life.'

'I'm very sorry to hear it. What was Sir Wilford talking about when you rode home from Tilberry together last night? Mr. Stormont told me that you and he rode ahead of the others.'

'We were talking about the commonest subjects in the world, uncle. Horses, races, Marion's adventure on Fixture, and the merits of Juno—the mare I was riding.'

'Humph! I fully made up my mind that he had taken that opportunity of proposing to you.'

'I am sorry you should feel disappointed, uncle. But I really don't understand why you should wish me to marry. It's not very flattering to me.'

'You ought to understand, child. My time is growing short, and I should like to see you established in a brilliant position before I go.'

'My position will be brilliant enough when I am in possession of your wealth,' thinks Sibyl, but she acknowledges her uncle's anxiety for her welfare

with a tender murmur, expressive of the desire that
he should live for ever.

Mr. Pilgrim comes out to the door to receive
Mr. Trenchard and his niece, and for the first time
in her life Sibyl touches his hand. It is curiously
soft and flaccid, and gives her an unpleasant sensation, as if she had touched some strange animal,
some member of the stoat or mole tribe.

'So glad to see you back!' he says to Mr.
Trenchard, in the blandest voice. 'I was afraid the
attractions of that fine old country house——'

'You ought to know that when I say a thing I
abide by it,' answers Mr. Trenchard, curtly. 'Mr.
Pilgrim, my niece, Miss Faunthorpe.'

'If you knew how I have been longing for this
opportunity, Miss Faunthorpe.'

'Don't waste time on compliments, Joel; Sibyl
will scarcely have time to change her dress for
dinner.'

Sibyl runs upstairs to her room, cheerful with
blazing fire and lighted candles—a very different
chamber to return to from that dark first-floor front
of Mrs. Bonny's, where one had to grope for lucifer

match and candlestick in the winter dusk. Yet so unreasonable a thing is human nature, that on this January evening Sibyl would gladly exchange these luxurious surroundings of hers for the one pair room in Chelsea, could the wheel of time make a backward revolution and give her back her husband's confidence and love.

This stranger's presence has impressed her disagreeably. There is something in her uncle's manner to Mr. Pilgrim, and in Mr. Pilgrim's manner to her uncle, that inspires distrust. The evening at Lancaster Lodge is very quiet and dreary after the life and bustle of the How. Mr. Trenchard and his Indian friend retire to the study after dinner to talk business, and Sibyl is left alone with her books and piano. She finds comfort in neither, and perhaps, were Alexis to appear before her to-night on the same errand that brought him to Redcastle a few weeks ago, she would exchange all her chances of wealth to follow his uncertain fortunes.

CHAPTER XIV.

ALEXIS COMES TO GRIEF.

THAT interview at Redcastle has embittered Alexis Secretan's feelings towards his mercenary wife. Love has given place to contempt. A woman who could set the hope of wealth against her fidelity to him is unworthy of another thought of his.

He goes back to Cheswold reckless, angry, wounded to the core of his heart, and he tells himself that he is indifferent to his wife's fate, that he cares not if he never see her false face again.

The blow that has hit him hardest, he thinks, is the knowledge of his boy's death. That son whose fair young face he has pictured in many a day-dream—seen vividly in many a vision of his sleep, —the son who was to inherit Cheswold in the days to come—the son for whose sake it would have been so proud and pleasant a labour to add field to field,

and extend the boundaries of that modest manor—
this unknown but fondly loved son is lost to him,
nay, has never lived save as the infant of a day
old. The chubby yearling, the bonny boy of two
summers, whose image, limned by fancy, has been
almost a living thing for him, has had no existence.

The loss of this shadow hangs upon him heavily.
He is no longer the gay young squire who enjoyed
the novel pleasures of wealth and social status. He
is gloomy and absent-minded, and avoids all intercourse with his neighbours, save in the hunting-field,
where he rides like a man who holds his neck as a
trifle not worth his care.

In this desolation of his mind he turns to two
sources for comfort—the first, his faithful friend,
Richard Plowden, whom he detains at Cheswold for
an unlimited period, to the peril of the Brompton
fernery; the second, his stable, to which he devotes
himself a good deal at this time.

His two hunters are considered the handsomest
animals and the straightest goers in this part of the
country, and his reputation is advanced among the
rustic population by his reckless riding.

'I know you'll come to grief some of these days, Alexis,' says the faithful Dick, who looks on his friend's proceedings with much dread. 'Blokus, the gardener, told me yesterday that you ride with what he calls a "plaguey loose rein," and that you don't know the country well enough to run such risks. I don't like that tall brute of yours a bit.'

'Not Bayard?' exclaims Alexis, who resents this abuse of his last acquisition, a fine bay horse, sixteen two and a half, and described at Tattersall's as the cleverest thing in hunters. 'Why, he's the best horse I ever rode. Such a mouth! You might ride him with a skein of silk.'

'But you see you haven't ridden many horses,' responds the prudent Richard. 'You're half a foreigner. You haven't been brought up like these country squires, who have spent half their lives in the pigskin. It is pigskin, isn't it?'

'Yes, Dick. And do you suppose I didn't ride when I was in the army, and hunt into the bargain? and do you suppose I didn't ride in the colonies, where a man thinks nothing of forty miles in the saddle?'

'I don't know anything about the colonies, Alex, but you weren't brought up to following the hounds, like these Hampshire gentlemen, and I feel wretched every day you ride that new horse of. yours, expecting to see you brought home on a shutter.'

'And if I were, Dick, would it matter to any one except you?'

'Alex!' cries Dick, reproachfully.

'Yes, old fellow, I know you'd be sorry, but not so sorry as the heir-at-law would be glad. Who is my heir-at-law, by the way? I must make a will, Dick. Some part of all these good things of ours must go to the only being I care for.'

'His wife,' thinks the simple-minded Dick.

Alexis rides over to Winchester that very afternoon, and is closeted for an hour with Mr. Scrodgers, the lawyer, to whom he gives instructions for a concise and simple will.

He leaves his real estate to his next of kin on his father's side who shall bear the name of Secretan, or, in the absence of any such Secretan, to his next of kin on his mother's side, exclusive of Mrs. Gorsuch and her children, who shall assume the name of Secretan.

'I feel myself bound to do this much out of reverence for the good old name,' he says, 'out of gratitude to my cousin Matilda, who honoured the name in my unworthy person. But my personal property I shall leave to the one friend whose sincerity I am assured of, and who stood by me when I was at the bottom of the ladder. I owe it perhaps to him that Miss Secretan's bequest found me an honest man, and not a blackguard or a swindler.'

'Very right, very proper,' murmurs Mr. Scrodgers, wondering whether he is to be put down for a mourning ring, or a legacy of a hundred guineas or so. He is old, and Alexis is young, it is true, whereby the chances of his inheriting any such legacy seem slender. But then Mr. Scrodgers is careful of himself, and these young men hunt, and drink more brandy and soda than is good for them, and shoot with new-fangled guns, and drive tandem with untried horses after dark. There might be a chance of his getting the legacy, should so proper an idea occur to his client. But Alexis furnishes his instructions without remembering the claims of Mr. Scrodgers. He leaves Richard Plowden all his personal property, furniture, books, horses, and pictures.

'They ought to realize enough to make that honest fellow independent for the rest of his days,' thinks Alexis, 'and now if Bayard makes an end of me some fine morning, I shall at least have done one good thing in my life.'

Mr. Scrodgers drives over to the Grange next morning in his highly respectable four-wheeled chaise, and the will is executed, but Mr. Secretan tells his friend nothing about its contents, nor is Richard Plowden curious. There breathes not on this earth a less mercenary creature. He is grateful beyond measure for his friend's affection, proud and happy that his presence at the Grange can give pleasure to Alexis. He plods on at his school books every morning in the snug quietude of the study, and in the afternoon takes long and solitary walks, while Alexis spends his days in the hunting-field.

The neighbourhood is full of rustic beauty, even in winter, and Richard, who has spent almost all the days of his life amidst a wilderness of brick and mortar, is delighted with these country lanes, these noble old trees, beautiful in their leafless majesty, these grassy hills crowned with dark pine trees, the blue river that winds through the green valleys, these peaceful English homesteads nestling in sheltered spots, and here and there a picturesque old water-mill, with a big brown wheel that never seems to go round.

Like many lame people Dick can get over a good deal of ground, and get along as fast as those who have the full use of their legs. He grows strong in this pure air, and gets young again. His complexion loses its sickly tint. Those transparent hands of his lose much of their delicacy.

'If you go on in this way, Dick, I shall find my refined and intellectual friend of the Brompton Road developing into a Hampshire chawbacon,' says Alexis, jocosely, as they breakfast together luxuriously, in front of a blazing wood fire, one hunting morning,—the master of the Grange arrayed in pink and tops ready for the day's sport, Dick in a comfortable suit of gray homespun.

'I do so enjoy your lovely scenery,' replies Dick. 'There's only one thing makes me uneasy.'

'Your mother——'

'No, it's not about mother herself. She has some extra good lodgers in the drawing-room floor, and is as happy as the day is long. What I'm afraid of is that she'll give the ferns too much water. Mother has such an idea of watering plants. She thinks the more you drench them the better they grow, and she's rather self-opinionated in those matters, dear soul. I tremble for my polypodium.'

'I'm glad it isn't any other kind of Polly you tremble for, Dick,' replies Alexis. 'What a close old fellow you are, by the way! you've never told me anything about your experience in that tender passion which makes fools of the wisest of us sooner or later.'

'Simply because I have had nothing to tell.'

'Nonsense! Were you never in love?'

'Never. I have admired feminine loveliness and goodness in the abstract, but it never came near enough to me to tempt me to fall in love with it.'

'Happy man!' exclaims Alexis. 'To escape love is to shun man's worst peril ;—

    'For soon or late Love is his own avenger.'

It is the middle of February, one of those days on which the mists of morning linger on the face of the land, as if they loved it. Gleams of sun pierce that silvery veil, and the westerly breeze seems rather autumnal than wintry. The two friends part in excellent spirits, Alexis riding off gaily on his covert hack, Titmouse, a pretty little gray mare. Bayard has been sent on before.

'How's the bay this morning, Joe?' asks Mr. Secretan as he mounts.

'Fresh as paint, sir, but I thinks as you did ought to have 'ad him hexercised a bit yesterday.'

'Nonsense, Joe! I don't care a straw for a horse when all the spirit has been taken out of him. That boy of yours gallops like the deuce when he gets the chance, I know. I don't care about having Bayard spoiled that way.'

'I hopes Bay-hard won't spoil you,' mutters the groom, as Titmouse carries his master down the drive.

'I hope you're not afraid of that bay horse, Marshall,' says Richard, when Titmouse and her rider are out of sight.

'No, sir,' I ain't afraid of no 'oss going, and I don't say there's any 'arm in Bay-hard. But the 'oss is young and silly, and my master—well, I ain't going to be disrespectuous to so good a master as him, or I should say he's young and silly too.'

'But he's a good rider, isn't he?'

'He's a good 'and at sittin' on a 'oss, Mr. Plowden, but there's summot more nor that wanted to make a good rider.'

This conversation, superadded to honest Dick's own fears, makes him feel rather uncomfortable; but when he has started on his rustic ramble the sun shines out of the mist, the west wind is so balmy and caressing, earth is altogether so lovely in her wintry garb, that Dick's spirits rise, and he tells himself that a bold brave fellow like Alexis is not the kind of man to come to harm in the hunting-field. It is your timid rider rather who is liable to misfortune.

So Dick goes his way, and his way of late has generally been the same way.

There is a tiny village about three miles from Cheswold—a village so small that compared with it Cheswold is quite an important settlement. This other village consists of a cluster of labourers' cottages, with whitewashed walls, thatched roofs steeply sloping, and long strips of garden which would be quite an acquisition to many a suburban villa. There is a queer little old church at which there is service every alternate Sunday afternoon, and there are a water-mill and a homestead with a farm of about thirty acres appertaining thereto. This mill is the chief feature of the scene, and it is to the mill that Dick has come. It is a picturesque old place, big water-wheel, gurgling mill-race, and placid pool. The willows that lean across the water look centuries old. The low white dwelling-house, with its steeply sloping thatch, its white plastered walls crossed and recrossed by timbers painted black, must have been here in the days of Elizabeth. The snow-drops peeping over the tall box border yonder are half a century old, and have spread and multiplied in the shelter of the southern wall. There is a roomy old porch with wooden benches, and it is in this porch that Dick takes his rest after his three miles walk.

It is about a month since he came here one biting January afternoon—the roads white with snow, the hedges loaded with a fine crop of icicles, the ditches ice-bound, and black as ink. On so cold a day it surprised him a little to see a girl of delicate and refined appearance at work with garden scissors and basket in the little bit of ground in front of the homestead by the mill. She was plainly dressed in a gray stuff gown and black apron, and wore a little scarlet shawl tied across her chest, but her head was bare—a very pretty head, Dick thought, with dark brown hair, that made a rippling line across the forehead, and was gathered in a loose knot at the back. He was not quite clear in his mind as to whether the fair gardener was pretty or not. Her features belonged to no regular type; her nose was neither severely Grecian nor commandingly Roman, but rather inclined to the *retroussé*, but it was an in-

offensive nose at worst. Her complexion, heightened
to a rich bloom by the nipping air, was a thing for
poets to rave about—for painters to vainly imitate.
Her eyes were dark gray, with thick black lashes;
her eyebrows dark and strongly marked; her mouth
beautiful, though Dick was not wise enough to know
it. He only saw that her smile was sweet, and his
chief impression was of a look of goodness which
pervaded the face—or so he thought. She looked
so amiable that he, the shyest of men, ventured to
address her.

'Rather a cold day for gardening,' he said.

'I don't find it so,' she answered, smiling. 'If
my poor arbutus can stand the cold, I don't think it
will hurt me;' and she went on snipping off dead
leaves, and smartening the garden by those little
touches which maintain order and beauty even
at a flowerless season.

'We shall soon have the snowdrops,' she said,
cheerfully.

'Ah,' said Dick, 'they bloom about this time of
year, do they?'

He had made himself acquainted with the habits

of ferns, but had very vague notions about flowers. The girl looked at him wonderingly, and then, as he walked a little way further, contemplating the picture of mill-wheel and water, she perceived that slight lameness from which he suffered.

'Would you like to rest after your walk?' she asked, timidly. 'You have come some distance, perhaps?'

'From Cheswold.'

'That's a good three miles. Our porch is quite at your service if you would like to sit down.'

She opened the gate as she spoke, and Dick walked in. He felt as if he could not for worlds have resisted the invitation, so he went in, very shyly, and seated himself on the bench in the porch. The door was open, and opened straight into the neatest, prettiest sitting-room Dick had 'ever seen—or, at any rate, ever remembered having seen—in his life. Everything was so bright and fresh, the brass fender, the cheerful fire, the old cups and saucers on the mantelpiece, the white ceiling, the painted walls, the chintz-covered sofa and chairs, the small round table with neatly arranged piles of books—not show

books, but looking rather like volumes in the daily
use of a student—and a drawing-board—actually a
drawing-board, the old engravings, the little cabinet
of shells in the corner yonder. All the furniture in
the room might hardly have realized five-and-twenty
pounds at an auction, but the general effect was
delightful to Richard Plowden's eye and mind.

The young lady—he felt sure now that she was
a young lady, in spite of her homely dress and that
lazy old water-wheel—went on with her gardening,
nailed up stray shoots here and there against the
plaster wall, and took no more notice of Dick than
if he had been a hundred miles away. Dick was
much too shy to make conversation, so he sat in
silence, lazily watching the girl's graceful figure
as it moved about the garden, in a pleasant
reverie.

Presently there came a sound from within—a
small shrill voice calling 'mammie.' An inner
door opened, and a little toddling thing, just
emerged from babyhood, came running out to the
porch.

At sight of Dick it screamed as if it had seen

lions, and stood stock still, paralyzed with terror—
a significant evidence that a stranger was a rare
bird at Dorley Mill.

The girl ran to him, took him up in her arms,
and smothered him with kisses.

'Mammie!' said Dick to himself. 'Then this
charming girl is a married woman! I didn't observe
the wedding ring.'

He glanced at the hands which were clasped
round the child. No, there was no ring there.

'What a dear little—thing!' he said, doubtful
about the sex.

'Yes, he is a darling little fellow.'

'Your nephew, I suppose?'

'No,' and the girl's cheek crimsoned, 'he's an
adopted child.'

This was all Dick ever heard about the boy. He
might have known more perhaps had he been curious
enough or audacious enough to inquire, but he was
neither. Yet he wondered a little, adopted children
being rarities, to have stumbled upon one in the tiny
village of Dorley.

He came to Dorley several times, finding this

particular walk the most picturesque of all his wanderings, and he rested for half an hour, or even longer, in the porch, while Linda Challice, he had found out her name in due course, sat at work in the pretty parlour and chatted with him pleasantly, quite at her ease. There was something about Richard Plowden which made people friendly with him at once.

They talked about the country, which Linda knew by heart, and about London, which was a strange and wonderful city she had never beheld. They talked of books and flowers and ferns, and by this time they had become as familiar as friends of long standing.

Linda had never invited Mr. Plowden to come beyond the porch, however. She was not quite sure whether her grandfather, a funny little old man, who was always in a floury condition on week days, would approve of such a step on her part.

And now, on this fine February morning, Dick makes his appearance, rosy with his brisk walk, and takes his accustomed seat in the porch.

'If you come to Dorley some Sunday afternoon,'

2

says Linda, after a little while, 'you can make grand-father's acquaintance. He's always in the mill on week days.'

'He seems a kind old gentleman,' says Dick, who had received a friendly nod from the little miller.

'He is kindness itself. There never was such an indulgent grandfather.'

'And you have lived with him——'

'All my life. My mother was his only daughter. She married an artist who came to Dorley to fish and sketch one summer. She was very pretty, they say.'

'I can easily believe it,' murmured Dick.

'Oh, much prettier than I!' says Linda, blush-ing, 'if you are trying to pay me a compliment. I have a portrait of her in my room, painted by my father. It was quite a love match, and I dare say people said my father had degraded himself by marrying a country miller's daughter, for he was what people call a fashionable artist, and might have [made a very different marriage. But they were very happy, and I believe my father was almost broken-hearted when my mother died a few months after my birth. I suppose he didn't quite

know what to do with me, poor fellow, so when my
grandfather and grandmother offered to take care of
me he consented to my being brought up by them
until I was old enough to go to school. I was a
sickly baby, they say, and that decided him. Well,
my good grandmother brought me down here
within a month of my mother's death, and it has
always seemed as if I was born here, for I can
remember no other place. My first memories are of
the garden and the mill—the big black wheel and
the foaming race—and those snowdrops growing
within the box border.'

'And you were sent to school——'

'Never. Before the school time came my poor
father had died in Italy. He had earned a great
deal of money at one time, but his reputation had
not lasted as long as his life, and he left very little
behind him. I never went to any school except the
little village day school, where I learned to read and
write; and if it had not been for the last Vicar of
Cheswold—a dear old man—I must have grown up
in ignorance. But one day when he came over to
see my grandfather he heard my father's name

mentioned, **and was** interested in me directly. **He**
was a **great** admirer of my father's pictures. He
asked how **I was being educated, and when he found
that** I was not being educated at all, **he** offered **to
give me a couple of hours' instruction** twice a week
if I would go as far as Cheswold Vicarage. **I was**
only too glad—for I was fifteen years old at this time,
and felt **the burden of my** ignorance,—and for four
years **I was that** dear old **man's pupil.** He taught
me Latin, French, and Italian, and gave me the best
books in his library to read. I owe **it to him** that **I
never wasted an hour upon a** worthless book. **He
was indeed a** friend. His memory is dearer to **me**
than words **can tell.'**

Dick listens with profoundest interest, and is
about to express his admiration of the good vicar,
when a noise **in the** distance startles Linda and him
It is the sound of several voices talking in excited
tones. Linda throws down her work and fol-
lows Dick **to the** garden gate. **A** labourer in **a**
smock-frock comes running round the corner, by the
brief **row of** cottages which the inhabitants dignify
with the name of street.

'What's the matter, John?' asks Linda; 'anything wrong with your children?'

'No, miss, they be right enough, but there's a accident yonder with some gentlemen hunting, a young gent chucked over an 'edge, among the rushes in that there ditch just beyond your grandfeyther's field.'

'Is he much hurt?'

'His arm's broke, and there's somethink wrong inside of 'im, miss, some of his internal bones scrunched, I'm afeard, for he's been a-spittin' blood like one o'clock.'

'What are they going to do with him, poor fellow?'

'The other gents is a-bringin' him 'ere, miss, and I ran on afore to tell 'ee.'

Dick is pale as death. Those terrible presentiments of his! have they been cruelly verified? He can scarcely find voice to ask the question,—

'Do you know who the gentleman is?'

'One on 'em said it were the young squire of Ches'old.'

CHAPTER XV.

FALLEN BY THE WAYSIDE.

YES, Richard Plowden's prognostications of evil are realized. Not quite so fatally as they might have been, however, for Dick had seen in a vision of woe the figure of his friend stretched on a shutter, pulseless, lifeless, the generous heart at rest for ever. The figure which the gentlemen of the hunt carry along the narrow path by the mill-pool holds happily the spark of life still, but so white is the face lying on the huntsman's scarlet shoulder that poor Dick, running out to meet his friend, gives a cry of horror.

'Is he dead?' he asks, distractedly.

'Not a bit of it. He's only fainted. I'm afraid there's a few of his ribs broken. Do you belong to Benfield's?'

Mr. Benfield is the miller.

'No, but I've just come from there, they are

getting ready for him. He's my dearest friend. Where's the nearest doctor?'

'None nearer than Cheswold. One of the men has ridden off after him.'

They carry Alexis to the pretty old house beside the mill, and up a single flight of shallow oak stairs to the best bedchamber, the freshest and brightest of rooms, with two broad latticed windows overlooking the mill-stream and the willows, with their background of green hills. A man might find worse quarters than these in the hour of distress. Even in the midst of his grief Dick glances round the room admiringly, and thinks what a treasure old Benfield, the miller, has in his granddaughter, for it is Linda's taste, of course, which beautifies his home.

They lay Alexis on the pure white counterpane, and Linda sponges his temples with eau de Cologne, until presently the heavy eyelids are lifted, and the patient looks about him wonderingly.

He recognises Dick, and fancies himself at home at the Grange.

This young woman in gray is one of the housemaids, no doubt. How soft and white her hand is! He did not think he had so pretty a servant in his staff.

'Well, old fellow,' he says faintly, and with a wan smile, 'you were right. Such a cockney as I oughtn't to go across country with your born Nimrods. Bayard's youth and silliness sent me flying over rather a stiff bit of timber, and I'm afraid Bayard himself is demolished. By Jove, it was a thundering smash! I wonder if I have any bones whole? I feel as if they were all broken up in short lengths, like barley-sugar.'

'Thank God you can make a joke of it,' exclaims Dick. 'But you mustn't talk. You've been spitting blood, you know.'

'I thought there was something unpleasant going on internally. How did they contrive to bring me home? I haven't the slightest recollection of the transit.'

'Home?' echoes Dick, puzzled.

'Yes. I am at home, am I not? Or how do I find you by my side?'

'By a fortunate accident, dear old fellow. You

are at Dorley Mill, close by the place where you fell, and in good hands, I am sure. And now not another word till the doctor has seen you.'

Old John Benfield, the miller, who has left his work on hearing of the accident, comes in at this moment, carrying a steaming glass of brandy and water, which he believes to be a specific for all earthly ills.

'Sup it up, sir,' he says; and Alexis is about to comply, when a firm hand takes away the glass.

'Not on any account, grandfather. He has been spitting blood.'

'All the more reason why he should have something warm and comforting,' says Mr. Benfield.

'You must get him some cold brandy and water, grandfather.'

'Very well, little lass, it's always for you to order and me to obey;' and the old gentleman departs to perform his hospitable duty.

'Dick,' says Alexis presently, 'I should feel happier in my mind if you'd go and see what has become of that poor beast, Bayard.'

'I'll go, Alex. But I execrate the brute. If I

were to hear that all his four legs were broken I shouldn't care.'

'Nonsense, Dick! The beast is only young and silly. We were both too ambitious—wanted to fly too high.'

Richard leaves the sufferer unwillingly, and goes in quest of the bay. It is not long before he discovers the horse, a good deal chipped and knocked about, but in no wise seriously damaged, in the stable of the one small inn which adorns Dorley village—a house which you would hardly recognise as one of public entertainment, were it not for a dingy board above the front door—said door having sunk into the yielding soil of Dorley in a despondent and one-sided manner.

Standing in the semi-darkness of a dilapidated stable, principally inhabited by cocks and hens, Bayard wears the dejected and hang-dog aspect of a horse that knows he has committed himself. He gives a deprecatory snort at the sight of Richard, and comports himself altogether in a submissive and even crouching manner.

'Ah,' says Dick, looking at him as ferociously

as it is possible for the mildest of men to look—
'ah, you murderer!   I wish there was a law for
hanging such as you.'

He hurries back to Alexis, and tells him that
the brute is all right.

'Not a bone broken.   He only broke your
bones, the beast.'

The Cheswold doctor comes presently, having
driven over at a slashing pace to so important
a patient.   Richard supports his friend during
the medical examination, which is slow and
painful.

The ribs are much hurt, one bone has been
pressed inwards, whence the blood-spitting.   It is
altogether a serious case.

'I should like you to see Krysis, of Winchester,'
says Mr. Skalpel, the local surgeon.   'I shall not
set the arm till to-morrow.   There is a little swell-
ing, and there's a slight tendency to inflammation.
'I'll send a lotion, which must be applied
continually.   You ought to have a trained nurse,
by the way.'

'I'd as soon have a ghoul,' says Alexis, at

which the surgeon fears his mind is beginning to wander. 'I detest hired nurses.'

'Can't I nurse him?' asks Dick. '**I'm strong** and wakeful, **and** I'll obey your instructions **to the** letter.'

'You might be of use undoubtedly, but I think a skilled hospital nurse——'

'Send me to an infirmary at once,' cries Alexis, peevishly. '**I won't** have a hospital hag near me.'

'See how the suggestion irritates **him,**' says Dick. '**Could not his old housekeeper** come over from the Grange?'

'That might do. Yes, she nursed Miss Secretan, I know. I'll call as I go home and tell her to come over.'

'Do nothing of **the kind,**' exclaims Alexis. '**I'll** have no old women **pottering about me till** they come to lay me out. **Mrs.** Bodlow's a **very** good soul in her place—makes an admirable curry, and fries potatoes to perfection; but I won't have her at my bedside in the middle **of the** night. I'd as **soon wake up** and **see the** witches in "Macbeth."'

'Nervous temperament, very,' murmurs the surgeon.

'Let Dick—my friend here—nurse me, and no one else,' says Alexis.

The surgeon gives way. The servant of the house will no doubt be able to assist. All may be well. It would not do to offend such a patient, and this promises to be a long business—a very long business—if it is to result in recovery. There is a possibility of the case being brought to a sad and sudden ending.

Mr. Skalpel takes Dick out on to the stairs.

'It is not a hopeless case?' falters Dick, almost breaking down.

'Hopeless, my dear sir! far from that. But I will not disguise from you that it is very serious. There are grave dangers. The greatest care is needed. Much must depend on the state of the blood. Mr. Secretan is a person of steady habits—or, to put it plainly, not a drinking man, I hope;— not given to the pernicious practice which our modern slang calls "pegging"?'

'Half a bottle of claret at and after dinner is about the extent of his dissipation.'

'That's a good hearing. We shall pull him through, but remember that good nursing is the main point. If you find yourself unequal to the task we must get a trained nurse—foolish prejudice, very—not old hags by any means. Many of them nice-looking young women.'

Downstairs Mr. Skalpel sees Linda, and inquires as to the possibility of assistance in the sick room.

'I'm quite ready to give my help, if I can be of any use,' says Linda, cheerfully.

'No one better,' replies the surgeon; 'it was your good nursing that got your grandfather through that bad attack of bronchitis last winter. He'd have been in his grave but for you.'

'Dear old grandfather!' says Linda, affectionately.

'But you mustn't over-exert yourself, you know. I don't want two patients instead of one.'

'Don't be afraid, Mr. Skalpel. Elizabeth will help me.'

Elizabeth is the maid of all work, a buxom girl

who seems to be in a perpetual state of expansion, for her gowns are always too small for her, a girl with a brickdust complexion, big black eyes like damsons, a double chin, and a countenance expressive of supreme good nature.

'Humph,' says Mr. Skalpel; 'I don't know about Elizabeth. Elizabeth has enough to do to take charge of that troublesome adopted son of yours.'

Rather a queer look comes over the doctor's face as he speaks of the child—a look of some feeling closely akin to dislike.

'Trot is never troublesome,' replies Linda, and again her colour brightens as it did when Richard Plowden questioned her about the boy's relationship to herself.

CHAPTER XVI.

GOOD SAMARITANS.

For many weary days and nights the patient fluctuates between improvement and retrogression. The business is a long one, as Mr. Skalpel prophesied. Alexis approaches that mysterious border-land which lies between life and death. Mind and memory are dark. He sees shadowy forms at his bedside,—sees the unreal more often than the real, knows not where he is or what he is, and slowly awakening at last, as from one long troubled dream —a dream of almost infinite duration and of wondrous variety—he feels like a child new born to life, seeking dimly to decipher the unknown characters of a strange alphabet.

Who is this with the gentle face, the mild and thoughtful eyes, shadowy hair, and soft white hands, who ministers to him so patiently, whose voice has such a soothing influence ?

Is it his wife? A flash of sudden hope quickens the throbbing of his heart; he tries to raise himself up in his bed, when a strong hand restrains him, and a familiar voice says,—

'Alexis, dear old fellow, be careful. Mr. Skalpel says you mustn't exert yourself.'

It is no longer winter. The lattices are open, and through the tender green of the willows smiles the blue April sky. Birds are singing—there is a perfume of violets in the room—blessed heralds of spring. Yes, there they are, violets and primroses on the dressing-table—violets and primroses on the little table by his bed. Oh, welcome spring— welcome sense of new-created life in his own frame!

'It was good of you to come to me,' he murmurs, with half-closed eyes, 'good of you to nurse me. All forgotten, all forgiven. We shall be very happy now, Sibyl.'

He thinks his wife is at his side,—a melancholy delusion, which makes Richard Plowden very uncomfortable.

'My dear Alexis,' he says soothingly, 'it is not Sibyl; we didn't know where to send for her. The lady who has nursed you was a stranger to you until the day of your accident, but if she had been your sister she could not have done more.'

Alexis closes his eyes with a heavy sigh.

'She is very good,' he murmurs resignedly, 'and I have reason to be grateful. I took her for my wife—a foolish mistake. I ought to have known better But I am afraid my mind has been wandering a little.'

He turns restlessly on his pillow, opens his eyes again, and looks wonderingly round.

'Violets!' he exclaims. 'How good of you to get me violets at this time of year! What a blue sky for February!'

'February!' cries Richard. 'My dear fellow, it is the nineteenth of April.'

'April? And I have been lying here——'

'A little over two months.'

Alexis feels inexpressibly shocked at this revelation. What! the days and nights have been passing, sunrise and sunset, moons waning, and he has been lying there like a log, or like a madman, full of strange fancies, and unconscious of the flight of time. This loss of two months seems to him in some wise terrible. It is as if he had been lying dead.

'I suppose I have been very ill,' he says at last.

'Very ill, dear boy; so near death's door that we have often feared the door would open and you would pass the threshold. Thank Heaven, we were able to keep you fast on this side. You have to thank Miss Challice for your life,—there never was such a nurse.'

'You forget that you have done more than half the nursing, Mr. Plowden,' remonstrates Linda, who sits with her face somewhat shrouded by the dimity bed-curtain.

'I——, nothing of the kind. I've tried to obey your instructions, but at best I'm a clumsy assistant.'

'You are the best of fellows,' says Alexis, stretching out his feeble hand to clasp his friend's. 'As for Miss Challice,' he continues, 'I haven't the faintest idea who she is, or how she comes to be interested in me; but I'm intensely grateful.'

He falls asleep after this, and slumbers peacefully

for some hours. When he awakes it is tea-time, the lattices are closed, and a young moon shines in through the diamond **panes**. A fire burns cheerfully **in** the old-fashioned fireplace opposite the foot **of** the bed. Firelight and moonbeams shine into the room, flashes of silver and gleams of ruddy gold light up the old furniture, the cups and saucers and **the** old silver tea-pot on the round table by the fire. They shine, too, on a quiet figure by the hearth, the graceful form **of** a girl dressed in gray, who has fallen asleep in an old bamboo arm-chair by the hearth.

'That's Miss——Whatshername, I suppose,' Alexis says to himself. 'Curious business, very. Where am **I, I** wonder ? This hardly looks like **the** Grange.'

He tries to raise himself **into a** sitting position, in order the better to inspect the premises. The process is painful enough to wring a groan from him, and the groan awakens his nurse.

' You mustn't do that,' says the gentle voice which has argued and pleaded with him so often in his delirium, but which seems quite unknown to him to-night. '**You** mustn't try to sit up yet awhile.'

'Not yet awhile,' repeats Alexis. 'I've been ill over two months, and I'm getting better—I believe you will. I am getting better.'

'You are much better—you are getting well very fast.'

'Oh, this is getting well very fast, is it? And after two months I am not to try to raise myself in my bed. Do you know, it strikes me that's getting well rather slowly.'

'You mustn't be impatient. The injury to your ribs brought on inflammation of the lungs. You have been in great danger.'

'And you—a stranger—have nursed me?'

'Not a stranger. Providence brought you to our door; you are our neighbour.'

'"Which of these, think you?"' murmurs Alexis. 'Yes, you have been verily my neighbour, in the Gospel sense of the word. How shall I ever thank you enough, Miss——.'

'Challice,' says Linda, as he pauses at a loss for the name. 'Believe me, Mr. Secretan, I need no thanks. My grandfather and I are véry happy to have been of use to you.'

'Dick Plowden says you have saved my life. Where is Dick, by the way?'

'He has gone to lie down for a short time. He has had very little rest of late, poor fellow. And now shall I give you some tea?'

'Yes, if you will be so good. I should like some tea.'

She pours out a cup and brings it to him, and raises his head upon the heaped-up pillows which sustain his weary frame, and puts the cup to his lips. It is a curious sensation for him, this awakening to life; curious to look into this strange face in the uncertain firelight, to hear this gentle voice, to feel the soft touch of these white womanly hands.

'If this were but my wife, it would indeed be awakening to new life and new happiness,' he thinks, and the thought that another can so minister to him while his wife treads her selfish way, ignorant of his pain, is very bitter.

'I think I could hold the teacup myself,' he says, and he makes the attempt feebly, with a tremulous hand.

'Capital!' exclaims Linda.   'How strong you
are getting!'

'Oh, this is getting strong, is it?' enquires Alexis.
'I should like to have seen myself when I was weak.
I must have been a pleasing spectacle.'

He falls asleep by-and-bye in the firelight, and
sleeps long, for he has at this stage of his illness a
wonderful capacity for sleep.   When he awakes the
fire is burning low, and the dim glimmer of a night
lamp suggests some sepulchral hour betwixt night
and morning.   Richard Plowden occupies the easy
chair by the fire.

'Where is Miss—Miss—Challice?' asks the invalid.

'In bed, and sound asleep, I hope.   She has sat up
night after night to watch you, Alex.'

'She is very good.'

'She is an angel, or as near an approach to the
angelic as one can hope to meet with upon earth,'
replies Richard, with enthusiasm.

'Who is she, Dick? and by what concatenation of
events do I find myself in a strange house, watched
over by a strange young lady?'

Richard explains.

'Indeed. This **is** Dorley Mill, **and my** fair nurse is the miller's granddaughter. If I were a bachelor now, this might be the opening **scene of** a charming romance. But I should **have** taken that young lady for something **superior to a** miller's granddaughter; she has an air of refinement.'

'She belongs by inheritance to the world of art. Her father was a painter.'

'Challice—yes, I remember, I have seen pictures of his. **He died young, I think.**'

'**He** did, and left this young lady an orphan.'

Mr. Secretan, finding himself able to sit **up** in bed, and **hold** a glass or a cup, during the **next two or** three days shows great anxiety to be taken back **to** the Grange. **He is** anxious to resume **the** business of life—to **see his** horses, his gardens, **to** be within reach of his library. He is quite horrified when **Mr.** Skalpel informs him that **he** is likely to be obliged to remain at Dorley Mill for three weeks or a month before he will be strong enough to bear the shaking involved in the easiest journey.

'You need not be in a hurry to leave,' says the surgeon, 'you have been well taken care of, I am sure.'

'I should be an ungrateful hound if I were to forget that for a moment,' replies Alexis, 'but I should really like to relieve this house of my presence; I have given so much trouble.'

'That is all past,' says Linda. 'Our only trouble was the fear that you would not recover.'

'Mr. Benfield must consider me an intolerable nuisance.'

'He does nothing of the kind,' says Dick; 'he is looking forward to your going downstairs as if it were some grand holiday.'

Alexis sighs. The comforts and indulgences of a sick room pall upon his active temperament. But he resigns himself to the inevitable, and Linda and Richard do their utmost to make his life happy.

Now that bodily strength begins slowly to return he suffers from extreme mental depression. He feels as if this coming back to life were something of a mistake, that it might have been better to have slipped quietly through the dark portal. He feels that he has nothing to live for, neither wife nor child. No kith nor kin, only the beaten round of a prosperous man's existence.

'I who have tasted the bitter cup of poverty ought to find contentment in prosperity,' he tells himself; but as the days lengthen slowly to their lingering close he is not content.

'He's dreadfully low-spirited,' says Dick to his assistant nurse. 'What are we to do to cheer him up a little?'

Linda sighs and looks doubtful; but in the course of the afternoon she brings up some of her favourite books, Shakespeare, Tennyson, Dickens, and offers to read to the invalid.

He is delighted. Any relief is welcome that will take him away from his own thoughts. He chooses the 'Midsummer Night's Dream,' and Linda reads at his bidding.

'We'll have one of the tragedies when I'm stronger,' he says. 'I couldn't stand "Hamlet" or "Lear" yet awhile.'

From this time forward the reading becomes an institution. Linda is a good reader, her voice round and full, her emphasis always intelligent. Alexis makes a closer acquaintance with Tennyson than he has ever made before now, and renews his boyish delight in Dickens.

In about a week after that first reading he is well enough to go downstairs to the cheerful parlour, but not without support from Richard's sustaining arms. There is no longer any talk of his going back to the Grange yet awhile. He knows his own weakness now, and is resigned to the tedium of a slow recovery.

'You are all so good to me,' he says, with tears in his eyes, 'I should be a fool to wish myself away from you.'

It is a sunny afternoon in early May when he goes downstairs for the first time. Linda has done her uttermost to make the room bright and cheerful. There are flowers, sweet spring flowers on the chimney-piece, table, and chiffonier; violets, primroses, hyacinths, narcissus, pale monthly roses from the southern wall. A fire burns gaily in the old-fashioned grate; for the invalid is chilly, and May sunshine uncertain. The invalid's couch has been arranged in the cosiest corner by the fire ; snow-white pillows, Berlin wool coverlet, knitted by Linda's own hands as a Christmas **present for her** grandfather. The brown wainscot walls are bright-ened with water-colour landscapes in a higher style **of** art than Alexis would have expected to find at Dorley Mill ; but he learns by-and-bye that **they** are all the work of Linda's pencil.

'What a pretty room!' cries Alexis, when he is established on his sofa, 'and what a pretty picture that water-mill makes against the blue sky! I feel ever so much better for the change.'

He enjoys the novelty of the apartment as much as if he had come **into a** new country, **and** . his spirits begin to rise immediately.

'Now I feel that I am really getting well,' he says.

It is three o'clock in the afternoon. Mr. Benfield **is to come in** at five to tea, and there is to be quite **a grand** tea-drinking in honour of Mr. Secretan's convalescence. The simple-hearted old man **is** almost as delighted at his guest's recovery as if the Squire **of** Cheswold were his son.

Linda seats herself in her favourite chair by the open window. Dick places himself by the foot of the couch. The invalid lies in a lazy silence, looking out at the willows and the mill-stream, and the green hills beyond. How lovely nature seems to him after his nights of pain and darkness!

Presently he hears a small voice calling 'mammie,' and a small hand making ineffectual attempts to turn the handle of the door. Linda runs to open the door, and the prettiest child Alexis ever remembers to have seen runs into the room.

He has soft golden curls all over his small head, rosy cheeks, bold brown eyes, and the open, confiding look of a child that has been reared in love's tender keeping. He clings to Linda's dress.

'Mammie, mammie dear,' he cries, 'Trot wants oo, Trot nenner sees oo now. Oo viz de genlamum?'

'The gentleman has been very ill, darling, and he wanted me more than Trot does.'

'Oo tell tory. Trot want oo allvis.'

'You had Elizabeth to take care of you, pet. Elizabeth is very kind.'

'See isn't. Me hate Lithabess.'

'Oh, you naughty boy. Look, Trot, this is the sick gentleman. Go and shake hands.'

'Me won't. Me hate the genlamum.'

'Oh, Trot!'

'Cause he keeps oo away from Trot.'

'But he won't do that any more, Trot,' says Alexis, delighted with this infantile grumbler. 'Come to me, my little man, and let's make friends. See what I've got here!'

And Alexis produces his watch, that unfailing resource of a man who wants to amuse a child.

At sight of the watch and jingling bunch of lockets and seals the little one's eyes open their widest, and he creeps a little nearer the enemy.

'I don't like oo,' he says, " but I'll look at oor watch.'

With this protest he goes close up to Alexis, and allows himself to be entertained.

'What a darling little fellow!' says Alexis. 'A nephew of yours, I suppose, Miss Challice?'

'No, he is no relation. He is a little boy my grandfather adopted.'

'How good of him!   The son of an old friend, I
conclude.'

'No.   We adopted him to save him from the
workhouse.'

'Ah, that is like you—just as you took me in to
save me from death.'

Alexis does not like to ask any further questions,
yet he would be glad to know more about this fascinating little fellow, who soon grows friendly and
familiar, and nestles his golden head in the invalid's
waistcoat, and plays with the seals and lockets.

Presently the miller comes in to tea, and the table
is spread with a simple feast, new-laid eggs, cream,
cakes of Linda's manufacture, and strawberry jam,
which Elizabeth, the maid of all work, secretly believes to be the best strawberry jam in Hampshire.

Trot sits up in his high chair at the table, and
behaves very prettily, though he disposes of more
bread and jam, and follows it up with more cake
than Alexis can suppose beneficial to his internal
economy ; but then Mr. Secretan has seen very little
of children and their ways.

Henceforward Trot is a wonderful favourite with

him. He allows **the little fellow to** come into his room at all times and seasons, he sends Dick **to** Winchester **for** a cargo **of** picture-books, and **Trot** sits upon the invalid's bed **for hours together** looking **at the** pictures, **and** demanding explanations thereof. **When the pictures have been** explained to Trot by Alexis, Trot insists on explaining them over again to the explainer, and lays down the law about them and philosophises upon them in a delightful **way.**

Never before has **Alexis** had any dealings **with a** child. **It is a new experience to him.** The little fellow amuses him for hours together. The thought that his own **son** might have grown into just such **a** boy as this seems a **bond of union** between him and Trot. **The** boy grows **wondrous** fond of him, and places him second only **to** mammie in his measure of love.

'Have you had Trot long?' **Alexis** asks one day of Linda.

'Ever since he was a **fortnight** old.'

'What a charge **for** you! His parents are dead, of course?'

'I know nothing about his parents.'

'Indeed! Poor little waif and stray. If you
were not so very fond of him I should beg him
of you, and make him my son and heir.'

'I couldn't bear to part with him. You are not
in earnest, of course, but even if you were, and
offered him the greatest advantages, I don't think
I could bring myself to part with him. I have
suffered so much for his sake. Perhaps that is why
I love him so dearly.'

'Suffered? But how?'

'Pray do not ask me. I cannot possibly tell
you. It is all past and gone now, and I try to
forget it. But it was very bitter.'

This sets Alexis thinking, and the thoughts that
come of it trouble him. He sees but one solution
of the enigma, and that is one which casts the
shadow of disgrace on Linda Challice. Can she,
this gentle, lovable girl, with her fair innocent
face, be something less pure and perfect than he
has believed her? The suspicion pains him as
keenly as if she were his sister or his plighted
wife. He lies awake for many a weary hour pon-

dering over this painful question. For a little while even his heart turns from poor Trot, who is distressed at finding his new friend less kind, but Trot soon makes himself beloved again. Whatever misery this little brown-eyed boy may have unconsciously occasioned, Alexis cannot help loving him.

CHAPTER XVII.

BITTER ALMONDS.

FROM January to May is rather a lengthy period for a friendly visit, but although the hawthorns are flowering in Redcastle woods, and May is nearly ended, Joel Pilgrim is still at Lancaster Lodge. He has taken up his abode there as if he meant to stay for the rest of his life, Sibyl thinks. She has grown tired of waiting to hear of his approaching departure. He talks about going sometimes, but never definitely. He must go back to India before very long, he says, and Sibyl languishes for him to fix the date. He goes up to London on business now and then, but returns in a few days, and makes himself more insufferable than ever.

Sibyl has never hated any one as she detests this man. His presence makes life a burden to her. The luxurious tranquillity of her existence, the reposeful days, the pleasures of wealth, are all

poisoned by Mr. Pilgrim's company, and yet he
treats her with the utmost politeness, with defer-
ence even, and obviously admires her to enthusiasm. This admiration is the most painful part
of the business.

'If he only hated me as I hate him we might
get on very well together,' thinks Sibyl; 'but, as
it is, the creature gives me the sensation of living
in a glass case with a boa constrictor.'

Mr. Pilgrim does not enter Redcastle society,
though the *élite* are quite ready to take him by
the hand in the fulness of their love for Stephen
Trenchard. Mr. Pilgrim is of a reserved temper,
and prefers the tranquillity of Lancaster Lodge to
the dwellings of strangers. He dines well, and
drinks deeply after dinner, but the wine makes no
more impression upon him than upon the decanters.
Mr. Trenchard and he are often closeted together
in business conference, but they never talk business
before Sibyl. She has a vague idea that Mr. Pilgrim is a merchant, and that his house of business
is in Calcutta, but she has no knowledge of his
merchandise.

One day Mr. Trenchard complains to her, and with some bitterness, of her coolness to Joel Pilgrim.

'I think I have been kind enough to you to deserve that you should be civil to any friend of mine, Sibyl,' he says, 'and yet you are positively rude to Mr. Pilgrim.'

'I am not intentionally so, uncle Trenchard.'

'Then your notion of good manners must be a very curious one. Nonsense, Sibyl! you can be winning enough, fascinating enough, when you please. Yet to this young man——'

'Young!' echoes Sibyl. 'He must be five-and-thirty if he's a day.'

'No matter, child, he is a young man to me. For him, I say—the son of my oldest friend—you have nothing but cold looks and insulting speeches. It is very hard upon me, Sibyl.'

'My dear uncle, I did not know you were so fond of this Mr. Pilgrim. I have fancied sometimes that his visit was rather a trouble to you.'

'I have been worried about his affairs now and then. The man himself is very dear to me.'

'Then I will try to be more polite to him, my dear uncle, for your sake.'

'I want you to try something more than that Sibyl. You discouraged Sir Wilford Cardonnel's attentions, for some inscrutable reason of your own —don't deny it, girl, you must have discouraged him for I know he was over head and ears in love with you, and now he only makes a formal call once in six weeks. You might have had the first position in this part of the world if you had chosen, but you did not so choose. I saw you fling away your chance, and I did not reproach you. But now I come to something that touches me closer. Joel—the only son of my——' he pauses with a curious smile—'only friend, Joel Pilgrim, a man of strong brain and strong feelings, has fallen in love with you. Not a butterfly passion like Sir Wilford's, mind you, to be blown aside by a breath of yours, but an enduring love. Now I have set my heart on seeing Joel and you man and wife.'

'Why should you be so anxious to see me married, uncle Trenchard? You wanted me to marry Sir Wilford, and now you want me to marry this Mr. Pilgrim, with Indian blood in his veins.'

'I wanted you to marry Sir Wilford because he could give you a great position. I want you to marry Joel because Joel is dear to me, and to see you two united would be to secure the happiness of the only two people I love.'

'Don't be angry with me, uncle Trenchard, but I had as soon you told me a serpent loved me as this Mr. Pilgrim.'

She feels that in speaking thus frankly she runs the risk of offending her uncle. For once in her life she is truthful. Her uncle is less angry than she had expected.

'Nonsense, child!' he says carelessly. 'You are full of prejudice. You must learn to think better of my friend's son.'

'Is he the son of that friend whose death distressed you so much, uncle?' asks Sibyl.

'What death? When?'

'One evening last summer, when you read the announcement in the paper.'

Mr. Trenchard looks at her curiously for a moment.

'Yes, yes,' he says, 'that was the man.'

From this time Joel Pilgrim is more open in his attentions. He follows Sibyl like her shadow, rides with her, drives with her, walks in the garden, plays billiards with her, stands beside the piano when she plays or sings, reads the books she reads, associates himself with every hour of her day and every pursuit of her life. She knows not what it is to be alone. She takes the utmost pains, in a quiet way, to let Mr. Pilgrim see that his attentions are odious to her. She never favours him with an encouraging look or word, yet he pursues his course doggedly, like a man who comes from a land where women's opinions and inclinations go for nothing.

People in Redcastle are not slow to talk of Mr. Pilgrim just as they talked of Sir Wilford Cardonnel. It is now evident to the mind of Redcastle that Sir Wilford has cooled and fallen off in his attentions, and that this Anglo-Indian, with his dark face and sleek hair—a real Hindoo, perhaps, some people suggest—is to be Miss Faunthorpe's husband.

'They wouldn't go out riding together if it wasn't a settled thing,' says Mrs. Groshen to Mrs. Stormont, 'and in *my* day it was not considered correct for a young lady to go out alone with her engaged husband. But young ladies are changed.'

'It's money, I suppose,' remarks Mrs. Stormont, thinking of the main question and not of details. 'I have no doubt this Calcutta merchant is immensely rich, and Mr. Trenchard wishes to unite the two fortunes. I thought Sibyl looked very unhappy the last time I called. If she had been allowed to follow her own inclinations things would have taken a very different turn. I don't think she ever had such a genuine liking for any one as for my Fred.'

'She didn't show it much in her manner,' says Mrs. Groshen, smiling amiably.

'She is not a girl to let every one read her feelings,' retorts Mrs. Stormont. 'What is that some one says in a play about wearing one's heart outside one's dress? She's not that sort of girl. But I know she liked Fred. I sincerely pity her, poor child.'

The Stormonts see less of Mr. Trenchard and his niece after Joel Pilgrim's advent. This strange guest of the old man's, who will not go out visiting, even to the best people in Redcastle, seems a stumblingblock to social intercourse. Mr. Trenchard has also taken to refusing invitations, and Sibyl is dull and spiritless, and is even losing her beauty, Mrs. Groshen remarks, with a touch of satisfaction.

'Those brilliant complexions go off so soon,' she says. 'I'll tell you what it is, my dear, you may depend upon it that things are not quite right at Lancaster Lodge. There's something underhanded going on there.'

'But what?' inquires Mrs. Stormont, bursting with curiosity, for the solemnity of her friend's countenance implies a spirit that has penetrated Mr. Trenchard's secrets.

'I don't know what,' replies Mrs. Groshen, in the most disappointing way, 'but I have an instinct that tells me there is something wrong.'

'There is an atmosphere of gloom in the house, I admit. I feel sure that girl is being forced into a distasteful engagement.'

So gossips Redcastle, and not altogether without foundation, for the gloom deepens in Stephen Trenchard's house, a gloom which is not to be enlivened by upholsterer's work in the way of gilding and crimson tabouret, or by luxurious dinners served on porcelain and silver, or by fine raiment, or any of the things that Stephen Trenchard's money or credit can buy.

If it were not for one wicked hope, Sibyl would assuredly fly the hateful abode that holds Joel Pilgrim, but that evil hope nerves her to remain.

Mr. Trenchard has been showing signs of rapid decay. The east winds of March and April have withered him. Dr. Mitsand talks less confidently of his patient's fine constitution, and urges extreme care. He expatiates on the perils of our treacherous climate, and suggests that Mr. Trenchard shall spend next winter in the south of France.

Stephen Trenchard has grown nervous and fretful. He complains of sleepless nights, and his failing appetite is obvious to all his household.

Do not these signs betoken the beginning of the end?

'I will stay,' Sibyl says to herself, and she fancies there is something almost heroic in the resolution. 'However loathsome that man makes himself, I will wait for the end. Perhaps his passion for me is only a pretence, after all—a trap to catch me. If he can prove me disobedient, or force me to run away, he may induce my uncle to alter his will, and leave *him* everything. That may be his plan—a deep-laid plot to ruin me.'

Robert Faunthorpe dines with his rich brother-in-law about once in six months, a purely ceremonial visit, which is irksome to both men, though uncle Stephen is very civil, and uncle Robert enjoys the unwonted gratification of an excellent dinner and rare old wine. On the occasion of his last visit, near the end of April, Dr. Faunthorpe sees so marked a change in his brother-in-law that he goes home full of it, and tells Marion that he does not think her uncle is long for this world.

'What a shame !' says Marion, meaning Sibyl's conduct, and not her uncle's decline; ' and here have

I been estranged from him all the days of his life. It's a hard thing to be plotted out of one's expectations by a designing sister.'

' My love, we have no reason to suppose that Mr. Trenchard will act unjustly in the matter of his will,' remonstrates the mild little doctor.

' Oh dear no, he has acted so very justly all along; never put Sibyl over my head, never dropped me after taking me up. Oh, of course not ! '

To satire so subtle as this Dr. Faunthorpe finds no reply. He only sighs gently, and comforts himself with a pinch of snuff.

Sibyl spends more time at the parish doctor's house just now than she has been used to do. It is the only place where Joel Pilgrim does not accompany her, and on this account it seems to her a haven of refuge. She is more amiable to Marion than of old, more friendly to Hester, more affectionate to Jenny. She feels happier—or at least more at peace—in the shabby old parlour, or the shabbier surgery, than anywhere else.

Jenny, enlightened by Alexis, knows her sister's secret, and is therefore a person to be conciliated.

She has sworn eternal fidelity, however, and has never given so much as a **hint of the truth to** Marion.

It is a comfort to Sibyl in this time of trouble to lay her weary head **on** Jenny's substantial shoulder and talk hopefully of the days to come, when **she and** Alexis are to **be reunited.**

'He threatened never to forgive **me,' says** Sibyl, 'but I don't think he will keep his word.'

'I'm sure he won't if you do your hair the new way,' answers Jenny, with conviction. '**It makes you look lovely.'**

On Sibyl's next **visit** Marion is full of Mr. Trenchard's declining health, and talks about his death as if it were a settled business, appointed **to** come off within a given time.

'You will be grand, Sibyl! Shall you keep Lancaster Lodge and the carriages? **If I were you I** should **let** the house furnished and go **on the** Continent. Travelling **is so** delightful, and **if** you wanted a companion you might take one of your sisters.'

'How can **you** talk so horribly, Marion?' ex-

claims Sibyl. 'Who says uncle Trenchard is going
to die ?'

'Uncle Robert says he's not going to live long,
and I suppose that's pretty much the same thing,
only a nicer way of putting it. Uncle Robert ought
to know, as a doctor. He generally knows about the
parish patients. When he says they're going to get
better they don't always do it, but when he says
they're going to die they always bear him out. He's
very lucky in *that.*'

'You are the most dreadful girl, Marion.'

'Well, you needn't colour up and look pleased.
That's quite as bad as talking horribly. I've a
franker disposition than you, and I say things
straight out. I suppose he'll leave Jenny and me
something for mourning, out of respect to himself. I shall have a corded black silk, thick
enough to stand alone. I always looked my best
in black.'

'Did uncle Robert think that uncle Stephen
looked very ill when he dined with us the other
day ?' asks Sibyl, thoughtfully.

'Of course he did, or he wouldn't have said it.'

We say what we mean at this end of the town. They're more polite above Bar, and the more they say a thing the less they mean it. Mrs. Stormont told me she had taken a tremendous fancy to me when she thought I was uncle Stephen's favourite.'

' Don't be so bitter, Marion.'

' If you had to have your boots soled and heeled twice over by a clumsy country cobbler you'd be bitter,' replies the injured Marion.

Finding this young lady's temper inclining to acidity Sibyl slips away to Jenny's favourite retreat —the surgery, where she finds the damsel seated on the hearth-rug busy at needlework, and performing wonders in the way of stocking-darning.

Sibyl flings herself into Dr. Faunthorpe's easy chair in a despondent attitude, and sits there in moody silence, much to Jenny's discomfiture.

' You might say "how d'ye do?" to one,' she remonstrates.

' I beg your pardon, Jenny. It was mere absence of mind.'

' Oh, that's what you call absence of mind above Bar. Hereabouts we call it rudeness.'

'Don't be cross, Jenny. I'm very unhappy.'   .

'I thought so,' replies Jane, astutely, 'you've come to see us so much oftener than you used to do, a sure sign that you are miserable. Are you un-happy about *him?*'

'About whom?'

'Oh, you know; my brother-in-law.'

'Partly about him, and partly for other reasons. I am worried to death.'

'But uncle Trenchard will die soon,' says Jenny, cheerily, 'and then all will come right. We shall go into mourning, and be great swells.'

'Jenny, you really mustn't talk so.'

'What's the harm?'

'You mustn't talk of poor uncle Stephen's death as if it were an event we were all looking forward to.'

'But we are,' replies Jenny. 'I'm sure Marion does nothing but talk about her mourning, and how she'll have it made. I'm sick of hearing of corded silks and para—— what's its name?—and bugled fringe. I shan't have bugled fringe; it catches in everything, and one can't help scrunching the bugles. It's too great a temptation.'

'Uncle Trenchard is weak and ailing, but he may live for years.'

'No, he mayn't. Not if uncle Robert knows his business. He says he doesn't think uncle Trenchard will last the summer out. And then we shall come in for anything he has left us. Won't that be jolly ! I'd rather he didn't die till the end of the summer The dusty roads would so spoil our mourning.'

'Jane, you are a perfect ghoul.'

'Oh, it's all very well for you to be grand and indifferent. You've had the use of his money all along. We are looking forward to coming into a small slice of it. If I'm not made a ward in Chancery and my money all tied up we'll have hot suppers every night.'

'Do stop that senseless chatter. Where does uncle Robert keep the laudanum ? I've a racking toothache.'

'That's why you look so miserable, I suppose. All the poisons are on that top shelf,' and Jenny points to the topmost shelf in the darkest corner of the surgery, on which the quick eye of Alexis espied the blue bottle labelled prussic acid.

If Jenny were not so deeply engaged with the complicated dilapidations of her stocking she would clamber upon the doctor's step-ladder and bring down the laudanum, but she goes on with her darning, and leaves Sibyl to get the bottle from its dusty repository.

· Sibyl ascends the step-ladder, and descends again with a bottle in her hand, takes an empty phial from a drawer, and pours some of the fluid from the larger bottle into it, dexterously and quickly.

'What a smell of bitter almonds!' cries Jenny. 'You've got the wrong bottle! That's prussic acid!'

Quickly as she starts to her feet Sibyl has re-ascended the ladder, and replaced the blue bottle in its corner before she can reach her.

'It's all right, Jenny. I know laudanum from prussic acid. What a fidgety, officious child you are!'

'I never knew laudanum to smell like bitter almonds,' remonstrates Jenny, unconvinced. 'Show me the bottle you put in your pocket.'

'I shall do nothing of the kind. Go on with your work, and don't be ridiculous.'

Jenny mounts the ladder, and examines the shelf that holds Dr. Faunthorpe's small collection of poisons. The laudanum and the prussic acid are in bottles of the same colour, but the prussic acid is inverted in a gallipot. Each is in its usual place, but Jane's quick eye perceives that while the laudanum bottle has its coating of dust undisturbed the dust has been rubbed off the prussic acid bottle.

'I hope you are not doing anything dreadful, Sibyl,' she remarks solemnly. 'Tampering with poison is a dangerous thing.'

'I have only taken a few drops of laudanum for my toothache.'

'Well, I suppose I ought to believe you, as you're my elder sister. But I can't understand that smell of bitter almonds.'

'All your fancy, I assure you, Jenny. And now let's be good friends, and have a nice talk. Don't try to mend those holes. I will buy you some new stockings the next time I go to Carmichael's.'

'You're a dear!' exclaims the volatile Jenny, forgetting all about that odour of bitter almonds.

The sisters seat themselves side by side in the window seat, and talk of the future, Sibyl's future, which means reunion with Alexis. They will be rich, happy. Jenny is to live with them, and have a pony to ride.

'And shall we have hot suppers?' inquires Jenny.

'What a vulgar child you are! Of course not. We shall dine at eight.'

'That's rather the same thing under another name,' says Jenny.

CHAPTER XVIII.

VILLAGE SLANDER.

THE days glide by at Dorley Mill. Oh how gently, oh how sweetly, in what innocent rustic delights, in simple, childlike pleasures, shared and sanctified by the perpetual presence of a child! The willows have unfolded their tender young leaves. The white blossoms of the orchards have come and gone like all earth's fairest things, too brief, too transitory. The lazy cattle revel in golden pastures; the pine trees on the hill-tops put forth pale green shoots at the ends of their dark old boughs. It is the time of buttercups and young lambs, trout-fishing, and all delights of early summer, and it has brought along with it fair nights and days, healing and strength, to Alexis Secretan.

Yet, strange to say, now that he is so much better, and nearly well enough to bear the journey to the Grange, he is no longer impatient to return thither.

'My life will be so dull without Trot,' he says. 'I'm afraid I have fallen in love with Trot.'

And then he sighs deeply, and lapses into one of those despondent moods which come upon him sometimes.

Linda bends very low over her work, and she too sighs, but so softly that the sigh reaches no ear but Richard Plowden's, who sits close beside her work-table.

Alexis is well enough to go out of doors and walk a little way, assisted by his cane on one side, and on the other by Linda or Richard. They take it in turns to accompany him in these brief walks; and Linda shows him all the beauties of nature to be seen within a few hundred yards of the mill. They all sit out of doors a good deal in the balmy June weather, and Linda takes her work and books to the rustic bench under the willows, and Alexis has many an afternoon nap, lulled by the babble of the mill-stream.

But the day comes at last when Mr. Skalpel,

who, if he has erred at all, has erred on the side of caution, pronounces that his patient is quite well enough to bear the journey home.

'And I do not say you could not have borne it a fortnight ago,' adds the surgeon, ' but I knew you to be particularly well off here, and one cannot be too careful.'

' Yes, I am very well off here,' says Alexis, with a smothered sigh.

' However, since you are well enough to walk the length of the village you are certainly well enough to bear a three-mile drive, and we have no excuse for keeping you here any longer.'

'No, I have no excuse for remaining,' says Alexis, thoughtfully.

' Six weeks ago you were in a great hurry to go home. I could hardly persuade you to be patient.'

' Six weeks ago I was ill and fretful. Since then I have domesticated myself here, and now I feel as if Dorley Mill were home. Mr. Benfield and his granddaughter are so good to me ; and this little fellow,' adds Alexis, laying his hand on the golden head of Trot, who lies at his feet with an open picture-book spread out before him, 'this little one and I have grown such friends that I don't know what I shall do without him.'

'Ah,' says Mr. Skalpel, waxing grave, 'poor little boy.'

'You speak as if he were no favourite of yours.'

'He is not,' replies the surgeon. 'He has caused too much scandal to be a favourite of mine.'

'What do you mean by scandal?'

'Well, Mr. Secretan, country people are censorious. It's a very unworthy feeling on their part, but you'll find that country people *are* censorious.'

'I have discovered the same failing in London people occasionally,' remarks Alexis.

'And if anything happens which is not quite open and on the surface, country people are apt to take a narrow view of it. Now Mr. Benfield's adoption of this boy has given rise to some very unpleasant reports.'

'Why should it do so? Is it not an act of charity, a most praiseworthy act?'

'Possibly, possibly, my dear Mr. Secretan. That is the way in which I have always endeavoured to see it, but one can't get other people to look at the thing with the same largeness of view. There is my wife now, an admirable woman ; Miss Challice was a great favourite of hers before the appearance of this child ; she would have done anything for her ; but since this baby came on the scene my wife has quite turned against the poor girl, will hardly allow her name to be mentioned in her presence.'

' That seems rather hard.'

' It is hard, but it is human nature. There are some sharp angles in human nature. It isn't all Hogarth's line of beauty. You see this child made his appearance in a most mysterious way. If he had dropped from the moon it couldn't have been more sudden, and we know no more about his origin than we do of a moonstone.'

'Then people have talked unpleasantly about Miss Challice, I infer.'

'They have, Mr. Secretan. There have been hard things said in the village with reference to that child. The village mind is coarse, and the village vocabulary is limited. Spades are called spades.'

'And your villagers can hatch a lie out of their foul imaginations,' says Alexis, in a tone that quite startles the placable doctor.

'I have always stood up for Miss Challice,' he says, 'I have always defended her.'

'I am sorry there should be any need for defence,' replies Alexis, sternly. 'I am sorry the people of Dorley and its neighbourhood should be such savages and idiots as not to recognise purity when they see it. I have lived nearly six months under the roof that shelters Miss Challice, and if she is not pure and perfect among women I have no power to recognise womanly purity and goodness.'

'I am entirely with you there, Mr. Secretan, yet I cannot help regretting that this child should have ever been brought here to occasion a scandal. There is a secret of some kind about his origin, and wherever there is a secret there is always food for slander. I am sorry because I know Miss Challice has suffered.'

'What, the slanders have reached her ears?'

'Yes, on some occasions, and they have made her very unhappy.'

'Poor girl! Yet when I offered to adopt Trot, she would not hear of such a thing.'

'I dare say not. The little fellow has wound himself about her heart, no doubt. They were always a soft-hearted race, these Benfields. The old man has been an encourager of tramps and beggars, too easy by half. It doesn't do, Mr. Secretan.'

'Benevolence? No, it seems a failure in this life.'

This conversation with the surgeon makes a strong impression upon Alexis. Instead of going downstairs to the sitting-room where Richard and Linda are expecting him, he remains in his own room all the afternoon, keeping the child for his companion. The little fellow will amuse himself for an hour together, playing about the room in his quiet little way, and perfectly happy.

Alexis looks at him with infinite compassion.

'Poor little waif, what is to be your fate in the years to come?' he asks himself. 'You cannot always have the calm shelter of Dorley Mill. The day will come when you will have to go out into the world to fight the battle of life—nameless, perhaps friendless, unless I am living to befriend you. Poor child, I would give much to know your history, and yet there are questions I dare not ask. There is always the horrible doubt, the lurking fear that this village scandal may contain some grain of truth.'

He is disinclined for Linda's society that evening, and goes out at sunset for a solitary stroll, with no support but his cane. It is the first time he has walked without the help of Linda or Richard.

He goes down to the willow-shaded path, contemplates the simple pastoral landscape in a thoughtful mood, scarcely seeing the objects he gazes at, and then strolls past that brief row of old-fashioned cottages which constitutes the village of Dorley.

Some men are standing before the little public-house, and one of them seems considerably amused in a quiet way at the appearance of Alexis, pale and wan still, and leaning heavily on his cane.

'He don't look up to much yet, do he?' says one of these village worthies when Alexis has passed, but before he is out of hearing.

'No,' says the man who grinned. 'He looks a rare sight. Yon's the rich gentleman at the mill. Miss Challice's new lovyer.'

'Who says he's her sweetheart?' asks the other.

'Well, folks don't say it, may be, but they knows it pretty well, I should think.'

'That's the young woman that's got the 'dopted child,' says the facetious man's friend.

The humorist is a drunkard and ne'er-do-well, who has been refused employment at the mill, and is bitter against Mr. Benfield and his household.

''Dopted child!' he says, with his coarse laugh, raising his voice on purpose that Alexis may hear him. 'There's many sech 'dopted children in these parts, but we calls 'em by another name. We calls 'em——'

He has just time to utter a blasphemous adjective, but not the substantive that is to follow it, for the adjective is thrust back between his teeth, as it were, by a blow which strikes him on the mouth and seems to loosen every tooth in his head. It is astonishing how hard a weak man can hit

when his arm is impelled by such passion as moves
Alexis to-night. He staggers from the recoil of his
own blow, and might fall were it not for a by-
stander's friendly arm stretched out to support him·

'Sarve him right,' says one of the sufferer's companions, as he stands before them, a piteous object,
pouring his blood upon the dusty ground, as in a
libation to the great mother. 'He didn't ought to
have gone and said anything agen Miss Challice.
She be a good friend to the poor folks.'

The injured man growls out some threat about
'summonsing' and 'the beak.'

'Summon me before whom you please,' replies
Alexis. 'I shall think this evening's work cheap at
five pounds.'

Alexis goes back to the mill curiously moved by
what has happened.

'Why do I feel insult to her so keenly?' he asks
himself. 'Is it that she is more to me than I dare
avow even to my own heart? Is there peril for my
future peace in this quiet home that has sheltered
my sickness and pain? Your fault, Sibyl, your
fault. You have left your place to be occupied by

another. Whatever evil befalls me is your work. Let it be my care that I bring no evil upon the good Samaritans who have succoured me in my weakness. Mr. Skalpel is right, I have no excuse for remaining at Dorley another day. But before I go I would give much to learn the secret of that child's adoption.'

He is not a little enfeebled by his act of violence and the passion that accompanied it. His heart beats violently, and he is barely strong enough to get back to the mill, where he arrives in a state of extreme exhaustion, and so pale as to frighten Linda and Richard almost as much as if his ghost had returned instead of himself.

'How ill you are looking, Mr. Secretan!' says Linda anxiously, when she has arranged the pillows on his sofa and brought him a tumbler of claret and water. 'You have been walking too fast, and alone.'

'I am sorry I look so ill,' replies Alexis, 'for Mr. Skalpel tells me I am quite well, and I am to go home to-morrow.'

'To-morrow?'

'Yes; there is no excuse for my being a burden to you any longer.'

'You have never been a burden,' answers Linda, in a very low voice. Her face is hidden from Alexis, but not from Richard Plowden, who in their daily companionship has learned the meaning of that thoughtful countenance all too well. He reads her secret there to-night, and the knowledge pierces him to the heart.

END OF VOL. II.

J. and W. Rider, Printers, 14, Bartholomew Close, London.

www.ingramcontent.com/pod-product-compliance
Lightning Source LLC
Chambersburg PA
CBHW021258050726
47498CB00003BB/897